MOTHER NATURE'S MERCY

A JESSE CLAYTON ADVENTURE

BOOK 3

DANIEL GRABOWSKI

Well Marie,
If you've gotten this far either you're enjoying these or you are incredibly polite — I'm grateful on both counts.

Enjoy!

Copyright © 2023 by Daniel Grabowski

Published by DS Productions

ISBN: 9798388227812

All rights reserved.

No part of this book may be reproduced in any form or by any electronic or mechanical means, including information storage and retrieval systems, without written permission from the author, except for the use of brief quotations in a book review.

PROLOGUE

"I think we should turn back," Otto said.

Dusk had crept up on them. The trees cast twisted and ominous shapes in the burning glow of his torchlight. He looked to his friend Kip, the butcher's boy, and saw the shadows dancing across his rounded face too. It reminded Otto of the moon.

"Quit whining," Kip said. "We ain't gonna be out much longer. It's gotta be around here somewheres." Kip was keeping his attention close to the ground.

Kip had hit a deer about a half hour ago. He wasn't that accurate with his rifle, now slung across his back, and his prey had up and run without a second thought to the bullet in its side. Kip had wanted to hunt and bring something back for his father. Otto wasn't quite so sure of the idea; the butcher already had plenty of meat salted and ready to sell.

But Otto was not quite used to these American ways just yet. And Kip was his friend. He wouldn't let him go alone.

It was dangerous to be alone.

The wind whispered through the trees and Otto felt its chill. His resolve was starting to wane. "We really should go back. Kip, please?"

"Nah, we'll be fine. There's two of us. Besides I got this," Kip smiled at him and then tapped the rifle butt with his head. "Ain't nothin' or nobody gonna hurt us while I got this. Come on." Kip carried on ahead of Otto, keeping his eyes fixed on the ground.

Otto had other ideas. His eyes darted with every new shape and sound. He wanted a drink. He wanted to go home. He wasn't ashamed to admit that he wanted his mother right now. Or how much he would appreciate the soothing logic of his father.

He carried on, willing forward his feet that now felt twice as heavy, worrying about falling behind Kip and what little safety his friend's presence provided. He wondered what his father might say in this instance. He would tell Otto to think it through, assess what was happening around him, and decide whether his fears were disproportionate to his actual circumstance. They had fire; that would deter almost any animal. The bears wouldn't exactly shy away, but that was what the rifle was for. If at first the sound of its firing did not prevail, the force of its bullets would. He felt the tightness in his chest loosen a little, and Otto let out a long, calming breath.

What about the people who never came back?

The question just appeared in his mind, a brutal invader that shattered what little confidence he had garnered with his thoughts. He clutched the torch in his hand tighter and quickened his pace. Those who hadn't come back to Bleaker's had had torches too. They'd had weapons too. But something out here had gotten them. The talk of the Creek was that Indians were responsible. That was what the trappers and mountain men had said anyway. They'd come back with a broken arrow once. Apart from that, there was no trace of the people or the perpetrators.

And yet, here Otto was, sixteen years old, helping out his friend but a year older, suddenly realizing how foolish he had been. Otto hoped he would get back, and he would savor the lecture he would receive from his father. He wasn't so sure if Kip was smart enough to be aware of the danger. Like his father, he often acted without thinking first. As he had this afternoon, and now the two of them were chasing a lost cause through the fading light.

"There's blood over here!" Kip said. He kept his voice low, but Otto could hear the emphasis in his whispered tones. "I'm pretty sure it's slowing down too. We can catch it yet, Otto. Keep moving."

"Kip, I—"

"Come on! A few more minutes and we'll have it. Then

we can hightail it back in no time!" Kip's monobrow sat across his eyes in a way that Otto knew he wouldn't be reasoned with. "What's the German word for yellow again?"

"Gelb."

"Don't go bein' such a *gelb-er* belly for once. Now come on." Kip took off walking again. Otto's shoulders dropped and he carried on after his friend.

After a few minutes of careful walking through the forest, they came up to a clearing. The two of them stopped. They took cover behind the trees as they watched the young deer limp its way across the open space. Otto felt a pang of sympathy in his gut as he watched its desperate and hampered movements.

Kip grinned. "I gotchoo now, you idjit." He unslung his rifle. He glanced up again to check its position before he raised his rifle.

An arrow struck it clean through the head. It dropped to the grass. The deer's legs put out a frantic and brief scramble before it lay motionless.

The two boys exchanged a glance. Kip's expression now mirrored Otto's.

A figure walked across the clearing. In the darkness, it was hard to piece together any real details, but Otto could see the tall man with powerful limbs and a long ponytail. He carried a bow, another arrow nocked and ready. The figure stood over the fallen deer. His head turned and looked over at them.

Kip moved to raise his rifle. An arrow whistled and buried itself into the tree next to him. He dropped the rifle and screamed. He grabbed Otto and shouted, "RUN!" Pulled off balance, Otto fell to the ground as his friend ran away back into the depths of the forest. He risked a glance back.

The figure was standing still, with his bow down by his side, looking directly at Otto. Icy fear seized Otto's chest, and the teenager scrambled to his feet. He plucked up his torch and took off after his friend.

It wasn't until he saw the lights of Bleaker's Creek that Otto realized he was screaming.

1

HOW'S ABOUT YOU KEEP ME FROM BLEEDIN'

Jesse's train ride to Missoula was a much more pleasant experience than his attempted trip to Spokane. It had been a lengthy and sprawling journey, stretching from northern Idaho and into western Montana, but he hadn't felt the long hours one bit.

He'd stumped up the extra cash for a seat in first class after his brief experience of it on that ill-fated train to Spokane. And boy, was it worth every cent to him. The padded seating, spacious booth, and table all to himself were all the more pleasant without the constant fighting and fear of ending up dead. Tiredness had taken to him quickly, and he'd drawn those velvet curtains in his window closed and tipped his hat to an old man across the car before tipping it forward to cover his eyes. He'd shifted a little to be more comfortable.

Then sleep embraced him.

~

He woke with a snort.

The whistle of the train had Jesse flinching in his seat. His Stetson slipped off his head and onto the table. He groaned as he stretched out his arms and legs, feeling the steady simmer in his muscles and the crackling in his joints. The sleep had done him some good, but he was still carrying plenty of aches, pains, and bruises from Eddie Bradshaw and his boys (and girl, he remembered).

The train was still. His car was empty. Jesse rubbed at his eyes and stood up, then made his way to the door of the car and the exit.

The light of Missoula stung his eyes and the crisp, cool air nipped at his fingers as he stepped off the train and onto the platform. Jesse thought Rathdrum had been big; Missoula's platform was double in length, at the very least. It was packed with people milling around, shuffling along down to collect their luggage, or just taking off straight for the exit and on with their day.

Jesse pulled his coat closed and slipped into the current of people exiting the station. It was nice to stretch his legs and feel the cold; he'd gotten terribly stiff. He couldn't quite believe he'd slept almost the whole journey. But then again, often after a beating he'd been known to sleep through the next day and a half.

He left the station and was again struck by the size of Missoula. The station was at the edge of what he assumed was its Main Street. It stretched farther than any he'd seen in the past few years (mainly because he liked to avoid the big cities) and structures lined either side. But even beyond Main Street, he could see the town spread across the plain. Not a canvas tent in sight, either. Numerous stables and more houses than he dared to count. Looming over the town like a steadfast giant was a mountain, its top capped with snow. He'd paused to take it in and thought Winona would have appreciated the sight even more.

But he wasn't here for Winona. He wasn't even intending to be here that long. He just needed to conduct his business and be gone again. On his way back to her. He took a deep breath of that crisp Montana air and set about Main Street.

As he walked down the road, his attention kept darting left and right. He passed saloons, hotels, two barbershops, a tailor, and a tool merchant before he finally happened across the first thing he was after — a general store.

Inside he went, a little bell jingling above the door as he did, and was greeted by the keeper. He was a jolly man with a mustache as impeccable as Frank's. It made Jesse wonder just what his old friend was up to.

"Hello there, stranger!" the keeper said in a jolly voice. "New in town?"

"What gave that away?" Jesse said.

The keeper chuckled. "I know all the faces from round here, plus that tired look on your face has me thinking you're off the long hauler from down in Idaho?"

"I think you're in the wrong business, sir."

Another warm chuckle. "Was I that close?"

"Like a barber's shave."

"Well." The keeper stuck his stubby hands into the pocket of his apron. "Tell ya the truth, I ain't no soothsayer. It's just that train always gets in right about now, and it ain't never late! And I don't think that'll go changing any time soon. It's always worth it for the look on your faces though!"

"Now you've gone and spoiled it," Jesse said with a smile. "A magician should never reveal his tricks."

The keeper nodded. "And that is why I'm in this business and not that of magic! Now, what's it bringing y'in here today?"

Jesse looked around at the store. Shelves were lined with canned food, vegetables, and fruit. Bags of wheat, flour, and plenty of other provisions were all stacked neatly along the walls. Behind the keeper was a rack of weapons; rifles, shotguns, and pistols, immaculate and proud, with stacks of ammunition boxes beneath. None of it was what Jesse was after, though.

He looked back at the storekeeper and said, "You got any paper?"

The keeper nodded and bent down behind his counter. A second later his head popped up and his mustache curled upward. "You want somethin' to write with too?"

⁓

Tucking the paper and pencil into his pocket, Jesse stepped back out into the street again. He went on down, passing yet more storefronts that he had zero interest in. He did spot a post office and noted its location for later. Not far beyond that, he came to a saloon. Big letters stenciled above its door declared it the Silver Spur. A touch bigger and nary a bullet hole, it was in much better shape than the Jewel in Fortune. Again, Jesse thought of his friend. Somehow, going into the Spur felt a little like a betrayal.

Jesse pushed through the doors and saw the impressive interior. A long bar, lined with stools, ran along the far wall. Above it was a balcony, over which almost a dozen women in varying states of undress leaned and watched Jesse. The saloon was pretty sparse. Plenty of tables sat empty. Two poker tables and a crapshoot stood vacant, too. Jesse surmised it was a little early for a crowd. Most folks would still be at work in a town like this.

Jesse approached the bar and sat down, ordering himself a whiskey. A stick-thin old man came over and poured it, using his free hand to scratch at the needly bristles on his cheek. Jesse necked the shot and then ordered another, and a glass of water with it. He took out his piece of paper from his pocket and unfolded it, putting it down in front of himself at the bar. He took out the pencil, licked the tip, and put it to the sheet. He lifted it again.

Eyeing the mark on the paper, it dawned on him that he had a lot to write about. Too much so for just a single sheet. From the moment she dozed off on the train, right up until he did so on his trip out here. Jesse threw back his other shot of whiskey, feeling the fire roar at the back of his throat and down into his belly. Hoping the drink would spark some inspiration, he thought, *Where the hell do I start?*

∼

IN THE END, he opted to keep the details light, figuring he could subject Winona to all the details—particularly of his selfless and gallant heroics—when he finally saw her face again. He still filled the sheet and half of its other side though, just with the summary of events and his intentions here in Missoula. He folded the paper, tucked it and the pencil back in his inside pocket, and finished the last of his water.

It crossed his mind to go back out and across the street to the post office immediately, to get the word to her as soon as possible. Jesse then had the thought of not being completely sure how long he would be here in Montana. He wasn't sure how far this Bleaker's Creek was, for one. Second, he'd still have to find Compton when he did arrive. That is, if he was still there. No, it would be best to keep the letter with him until he was almost leaving this place himself. It would be just his luck to send that letter and then end up delayed further.

Jesse got up from his stool and looked at the bartender. "'Scuse me, friend?"

The old bartender grunted with a nod.

"You heard of a place round here by the name of Bleaker's Creek?"

"Aye," the bartender said in an accent that wasn't American. Jesse wasn't sure what it was, though. It was more of a bark than a voice. "To the north."

"Is it far?"

"Well, y'ain't walkin' it." He wiped a glass with a rag that was an unsettling shade of brown. "Miles it is."

Well, at least the place existed. That was a positive start.

"Outside. Tek a left, carry on t' the stables. Coaches there. One of 'um will tek yer."

"Thanks," Jesse said.

The bartender grunted and waved his rag. Jesse took that as a goodbye and left.

Outside, he followed the bartender's instructions and did come up on a stable. Outside was only one stagecoach that looked fit to travel. With a pair of horses at the front, thick wheels, and a pair of windowed doors on the side, it bore the wear and tear of years of travel. In Jesse's experience, that was a good sign of reliability. If a coach looked too new, you couldn't be sure how long it could last out there on the road.

"Can I help you?" said a man with thick sideburns and frizzy hair pulled back by the goggles across his forehead. He'd stepped out from behind the coach and now leaned against it. His face was tanned and lined, the hallmarks of a man spending the majority of his days outside. The cuffs of his duster were pulled back, and the bottom of it was caked in mud along with his boots.

"Looking for a ride to Bleaker's Creek. Know where I might find one?"

The man raised a fingerless-gloved hand and pointed to himself. "You can find one right here, sir. Matter of fact, I'm about to head out there. Gots a delivery to make up there today. You armed?"

Jesse nodded and shifted his coat to reveal his Colt Peacemaker.

The coach driver clicked his fingers. "Excellent! Dixie Rhodes at your service!" Dixie reached out a hand which Jesse shook. "Normally, I would charge, but by God have you stumbled upon this here coach at just the opportune moment." Dixie pointed at Jesse's hip. "Now, you can shoot real good with that there thing, yaw?"

"I don't often miss, no."

Another click of the fingers. "Yaw! Yes, now! I like that. Okay, I got some valuables up in this coach, and there's been a few... occurrences up by the Creek as of late. So normally, I'd be takin' on my partner in there..." Dixie nodded at a man in the stable laid out over a stack of hay, "...for an extra pair of eyes an' a shooter. But with you, well how's about you keep me from bleedin' and I'll see you right up to the Creek with no charge? Not a single cent. That sound like a fair shake to you? Sure as hell does to me, yaw."

"Sounds fair. When do we ride?"

"That depends. You ready now?"

"Sure am."

A double click of the fingers this time. "Well, then, let's get going now while we got the bulge o' the sun. You hop up shotgun there, yaw."

Jesse rounded the stagecoach, and as he did, he heard Dixie shout to his partner something about not needing him. His partner just snored in response. Jesse pulled himself up onto the stagecoach and sat himself down. He noted the shotgun next to him. By the looks of the handle, Jesse judged it to be a double barrel; not bad at range, devastating in close quarters.

Dixie hopped up next to him and grabbed hold of the reins. "All right, now..." Dixie started and then raised his silver shrubs of eyebrows. "What's your name, son?"

"I'm Jesse."

"Jesse what?"

"Clayton."

"All right now, Jesse Clayton, if y'all are ready, lets' gitty-up, yaw!" Dixie said. He whipped the reins and whooped as his horses sprang into a trot. Jesse wondered if putting up with Dixie Rhodes would be worth the free ride. He just hoped it wasn't going to be too long a trip.

2

WELCOME TO BLEAKER'S CREEK

Dixie wouldn't shut up the whole way. Across the dirt roads bracketed with thickets of trees, up and down the swells of hills and across a river, the man just kept jabbering. And 'yaw'-ing. Jesse didn't even think the man was talking to him, just rattling off words like a Gatling gun. It was on the third separate occasion when Dixie started talking about the weird lump he had on his foot, that Jesse decided he would just go right ahead and ignore the man.

He'd taken in his surroundings and realized that they were traveling through one great forest. Trees dominated the land right up the mountains, all turning in their colors too; ambers, oranges, and browns, as if the forest had been gently roasted. The beautiful signs of fall were there for all to see. There was a clearing here and there, and a break in the woodland where the water cut through it.

"Whoa," Dixie said. He jerked up on his reins and the horses dug their hooves into the mud, jostling the wagon to a stop. Jesse's hand reached for the handle of the shotgun.

"Problem?" Jesse asked.

"Maybe. You see that tree line up there, up on that rise?" Dixie said as he pointed to a heavily treed hill to the right of the road, a few hundred yards away. Jesse looked, but all he could see were trees and shadows on a carpet of dead leaves.

"I don't see anything."

"Keep watching."

Jesse did. He let his eyes adjust to the distance, waiting to see what had gotten Dixie all pent up. Then he saw it. A breeze had stirred up the trees and the leaves, disrupting the shadows, and casting light on the figure of a man. It was as if he'd just appeared, materializing from the very shadows.

The figure was a fair distance away, but Jesse's eyes were good. The huge frame, broad shoulders, and limbs couldn't be anything but a man's. A long ponytail lolled across his shoulder. It could have been braided but it was too far away to tell—and Jesse didn't fancy himself getting any closer right then—but he could see for sure the bow across his back, and the blade about as long as his thigh tucked by his side.

"Is he—" Jesse began.

"An Injun? Yep. Seem to be a few pushin' this way these days. Is what I heard anyway, yaw."

"What's he doing, watching us like that?"

"Just that. Watching. Most likely seeing if we're worth hunting. Bleaker's has had some trouble with folks going missing," Dixie said. He waved at the 'Injun.' "Right about when we started seein' 'em."

"How many you been seein'?" Jesse asked, not taking his eyes off the unmoving figure.

"Me? Just him. Can't make a run down here without seeing him. Usually, he's a mite closer."

"Maybe he doesn't like me."

"How do you figure that? He don't know you was comin'."

"Just because you can't always see him, Dixie, it doesn't mean he ain't always watching," Jesse said. At that, the breeze rolled in again, throwing around leaves and shaking the trees. Once it settled down, the man was gone.

"Oh, that just gives me the shivers ever' damn time, yaw?" Dixie said, snapping the reins and getting them going.

"I can imagine," Jesse said. He kept his eyes on that tree line, watching the shadows and seeing nothing. He'd crossed Cheyenne and Navajo before, and knew much better than to believe his eyes. With them, there was always much more to things than met the eye. They knew this land a lot better than he and every other pioneer.

After all, they were here first.

~

"HERE Y'ARE, JESSE," Dixie said as he pulled up the coach. "Welcome to Bleaker's Creek. Halfway to the ass-end of *Nowhere*."

Dixie had a point. Tucked away from the road, Bleaker's Creek looked like little more than a camp, let alone a town. Trees had been felled to make space for a few log shacks that scattered the area. In the middle of them, one stood bigger than all the rest, its slanted roof giving it the look of a flattened hat. In front of it was the town square, a big opening in the mud that a few folks were walking through. It reminded Jesse of the Mabin mine, only damper.

Dixie glanced at Jesse and said, "Not impressed, huh?"

"Was it that obvious?"

"Sure, Bleaker's is small, a little rough round the edges. But there's good people here. Red, the butcher, now he ain't too smart but you go and give him a deer and he'll show you jus' how good he is with that blade o' his. See the big building at the back end there, yaw?"

Jesse nodded.

"That's the inn. Yer stay there, Greta will look after you. Don't be scairt of the accent, she's a doll. And her husband's the smartest man I know. But hell, you'll find that out for yourself soon enough. Off ya get, I gotta go deliver this."

"Thanks for the ride," Jesse said and started to get off before Dixie pulled him back.

"I don't know what yer business is here, Jesse, but I like you. Whatever y'all do, stick to the Creek, and *don't* go wandering off by your lonesome. Just ain't safe, yaw."

"Thanks to our friend up on the hill, right?"

"That's it. You take care now."

"I will," Jesse said and hopped off the coach and waved to Dixie as he rode away.

The late afternoon had brought on a chilly wind and the sun had thrown in the towel for the day, having already dipped behind the mountains. Jesse walked down the dirt path and into Bleaker's Creek. He passed a few residents: two kids playing in the road took a wide berth of him once they caught sight, while a woman sat in front of her house with muddy hands right up to her elbows and watched him with beady eyes. She scrubbed at her vegetables, and Jesse greeted her. She did not return his wave.

The locals look real friendly, at least.

Jesse went on, making his way into the square, and headed for the inn, signposted just across the open patch of mud. Again, people stayed clear of him, regarding him with narrow and suspicious eyes. Jesse had been to places before where the residents weren't all too trusting, but something about Bleaker's was different. Maybe it was the trees all around them, almost closing them off from the rest of the world. It gave the Creek a distinct sense of isolation. Maybe these folks had only ever seen each other. Outsiders might not be held in high regard.

What was it Dixie had said about the troubles they'd been having lately? Any kind of problem was enough to get anybody's back up when it came to strangers. Jesse offered up his manners, tipped his hat, and smiled as much as he could. He also kept his hands as far away from his hips as he could without looking a fool about it.

Jesse reached the inn. No signage out front with a name or saying it was, he just had the say-so of Dixie. Jesse tried to peer through the window on the door but it was all fogged up. He welcomed the idea of warmth and stepped inside, being sure to close the door behind him.

The heat welcomed him like an old friend. Warm air wrapped its arms around him in a toasty embrace. A fireplace crackled on the far wall, bathing the big open living space in orange light. A few tables set for dining dotted the room, and the wooden floor was scuffed and dirty.

"Hallo," a woman said from behind a counter to his right. She was taller than Jesse and had a slender frame clad in a simple dress, fitted with an apron. Her face was dominated by her long, hooked nose on which her spectacles rested. She glared over the top of them at Jesse, a stare not quite as intense as that of the rest of the townspeople he'd met, but by no means friendly either. One of her hands was under the counter in a way that gave Jesse pause. It made him wonder if in her hand was the grip of a shotgun, her finger on its trigger.

Jesse made a conscious effort to keep his hands raised.

"Would you like a room?" she said. Curt and swift to the point of being blunt, her accent was one Jesse couldn't place. "Would you like a room?" she repeated when Jesse didn't answer.

He approached the counter and said, "Yes, please that would be great. Thank you."

"Sign *zis*," she said, pushing the ledger and pen across the counter to him. The way she said 'this' had him wondering. He'd heard somebody say it like that before. A foreign feller, sure, but from where he couldn't quite recall.

"That accent. Where's it from?" Jesse asked, flashing her a smile he imagined would work for Eddie Bradshaw. Her frown deepened as she pushed up her glasses.

Well done, Clayton, now she's lookin' down her nose at you.

Jesse signed the ledger and handed over some money to secure the room for the next few days. He had a feeling if everybody in Bleaker's Creek was like the people he'd met thus far, he was probably going to need even longer than that. The thought of being here for the long haul did not appeal to him, especially with winter on the horizon. Jesse didn't imagine that this place would be very hospitable when the temperature dropped.

"Mr. Clatton. Your key," said the woman, a key resting in the palm of her wrinkled and bony hand.

He took it. "It's *Clayton*, ma'am. And thank you."

"You're welcome, Mr. Clay... ton," she said. She didn't smile, but the gesture alone was enough to give Jesse some hope.

He decided to try his luck. "Ma'am, do you know a man by the name of Lonnie Compton?"

Her frown deepened again and then she slowly shook her head. "I do not, no. Apologies, Mr. Clayton."

Jesse smiled, more at his bad luck than the innkeeper. "That's okay. Was worth a shot."

"Mein husband. He would know."

"Your husband?" Jesse asked. "Is he around here?"

"Ya." She rounded the counter and brushed past Jesse. She pulled open the door and yelled "DIETER!" She then carried on shouting something else, but Jesse had no idea what the words coming out of her mouth were. The woman closed the door, then rounded the counter again and waited without a word. Jesse looked around awkwardly, not quite sure of what to do with himself. He was happy she had both hands above the counter this time. It seemed he'd convinced her she wouldn't need to riddle him with buckshot after all.

The door opened, and in stepped a man in a tweed suit, patched at the elbows and frayed at the shoulders. He wore spectacles too, only the eyes behind his looked much more trusting and friendly. Bags sagged beneath them, and the lines on his face told a story of wisdom as opposed to hardship. The way his white hair had almost been tamed by the running of a comb, and his equally controlled mustache, gave the man a look of intelligence.

"Hallo," the smart old man said. He had that funny accent like hers, but much softer. "My name is Dieter Kraus. Welcome to Bleaker's Creek." He bowed his head slightly.

"Hi," Jesse said.

"Apologies if my wife was a little—how you say?—*short* with you. Normally, she doesn't deal with guests first-hand."

"Can't imagine why," Jesse said.

Dieter laughed. It sounded more like a cough to Jesse. "She didn't aim ze shotgun at you, did she?"

Jesse glanced back at the woman. "Not *quite* at me, no."

Dieter nodded. "Again, apologies, my friend. Hopefully, the rest of your stay here won't be as... stand-offish? Is that how you say it?"

"I suppose you could. Not from around these parts, are you?"

"Ah," Dieter clicked his fingers. "I could say the same of you, good sir."

"True," Jesse conceded, "but I at least sound like most folks here."

"You noticed the accent. Fortunately, in my profession, I

have been able to refine it a little more than my wife, but still, I have a ways to go. I am from ze Deutschland, or as you say, *Germany*."

"Can't say I know much about it."

"Isn't much to say. Otherwise, I wouldn't be here!" Dieter laughed at himself. "Speaking of being here, what is it that brings you to Bleaker's, Mister... ?"

"Jesse Clayton."

"Pleased to meet you, Jesse."

"I'm here 'cause I'm lookin' for someone. And I got reason to believe he's somewhere in your town, Dieter."

Dieter nodded. "Ya, ya. Who?"

"You know a Lonnie Compton?"

"*Nein*," Dieter said. After a brief pause, he added, "No." His mustache lifted in an apologetic smile. "The old tongue still slips from time to time." He shook his head and moved to the door. "I'm afraid I do not know the man personally, but I believe I haff heard the name before. I'm sure of it. I cannot be of any more help, but please..." Dieter opened the door and gestured for Jesse to go through. Jesse glanced back at the crackling fire and its comforting warmth. "I believe Red, our butcher, may have an answer for you."

~

THE CLEAVER SLASHED DOWN, severing the chicken's head. "Lonnie Compton? Yeah, I know him," Red said as he tossed the head down to his side and picked up the bird, leaving his cleaver stuck in his cutting board. His shirt and apron were covered with blood, new and old. He plucked at the chicken, sticking his tongue through the gap in his chipped front teeth as he did. "What's it to yer?"

Jesse eyed the man. He had greasy, tied-back hair and a bristled face. His eyes were almost as suspicious as Greta's. People here weren't quick to trust, Dieter seeming to be the exception that proved the rule. "He might know somebody I'm looking for."

"And who's that?"

"Nobody you need to worry yourself with," Jesse said.

"Won't worry myself with you, then," Red said and dropped the chicken onto the board.

"Red, you're being nosy," Dieter added. The butcher looked at Dieter, popping out his thick bottom lip.

"He good?" Red asked.

"I haff no idea. But he hasn't shot anybody."

"And Greta ain't gone 'n' shot him none either," Red chuckled. Jesse didn't see the funny side of that, but Dieter did. He picked up a rag that was anything but clean and wiped off his fingers. "All right. If you say he's good, Doc, that's good enough for me."

Jesse turned to Dieter. "You're a doctor?"

Dieter nodded humbly.

"All the way out here?"

"Ya. You'd be amazed how often my skills are put into practice," Dieter said, his eyes slowly drifting toward Red.

The burly butcher flipped him the bird. He then turned his head and yelled, "Kip! Get yer ass in here and finish this chicken!" A lanky boy, no more than sixteen by Jesse's guess, appeared from the back of the tent. Blond-haired and thick-jawed, he eyed Jesse with a scowl from the relative safety behind his dad. Red repeated himself about the chicken.

"Why, Daddy?"

"'Cause I got business with the Doc and you got business doin' as you're told unless you wanna be endin' up like that chicken. You hear?"

Kip nodded furiously and picked up the dead bird.

Red untied his disgusting apron and tossed it at his son, covering his head. The big man then stepped out from his butcher's tent as his son wrestled himself free of the apron. Standing to his full height, Jesse thought, Red could give Big Dan a run for his money in the size department. Maybe even Slim Joe. "Come on, let's get a drink and I'll tell y'all about it."

"I appreciate the offer of a drink, but I'd just as soon be on my way."

Red laughed. "You ain't gonna be on your way tonight, drifter. Not unless you can see in the dark."

∼

"Lonnie keeps hisself to hisself up in his cabin," Red said. He pinched his glass of whiskey between two thick and grubby fingers and loosed it down his throat. He let out a growling sigh as the liquid burned his throat and belly. He then continued, "Only takes delivery of meat from me. I send it up through the sellers who come through here. Once or twice, I've sent Kip. He's managed to not screw that up." Red told his story to the two of them, as they all sat at the table in the inn, backs to the fire. Across from them, Greta swept the floor, eyeing Jesse suspiciously from time to time. When he'd seen her doing it, he'd smiled and raised his glass to her.

"He been there lately?"

"Nope." Red shook his head and poured himself another whiskey. "Besides, I wouldn't send him right now. What with it being almost hibernation season for the grizzlies. They don't shit, and all they want is to eat. And whatever it is huntin' people up and around these mountains as well? Too dangerous." Red followed up that last part with a nervous chuckle.

"Dixie said something about that. People disappearing?"

"Ya," Dieter said. "The past few months, four people have gone out into the woods and not returned. We've found things. Clothing, weapons..." He paused to take a sip of his beer. "...blood."

"It ain't been good, that's fer sure. It's why folks round here won't be takin' kind to you, Jesse."

"Can't say I blame them," Jesse said, then leaned forward onto his elbows perched on the table. "Ya'll got no idea what it is? Not Cheyenne?"

"You've seen ze wanderer, then?" Dieter asked.

"Might've spied him coming in."

"Whatever he is, he ain't Cheyenne. Not this far north. My money's on that son of a bitch, though. Bears'd leave a lot more mess," Red said.

"Another reason why you won't be traveling tonight. Or alone," Dieter added.

"Yup, Compton is tucked away up the mountain. It's about a day's trip there and back. Unless you get a wagon," Red said.

"Oh, I think I have that taken care of," Dieter said.

Jesse paused, whiskey glass to his lips, and cocked an eyebrow. "How so?"

"You're not the only guest at the inn currently, Jesse," Dieter said with a mischievous smile. "I believe you may be able to help each other."

3

SOMETHING YOU SHOULD SEE

A knock at the door pulled Jesse from his slumber. His grip tightened around his Colt Peacemaker. It loosened as he became fully aware of himself and where he was. He sat up on the hard mattress and threw off the blanket. Instantly, he regretted it.

The cold of Bleaker's Creek had crept into the modest bedroom. Its teeth nipped at his bare skin and made his breath cloud the air. Tentatively, Jesse reached out a shivering arm for his clothes hung on the chair beside the bed.

The knock at the door came again.

Jesse got up, clothed as best he could with numb hands, and opened the door. He was greeted by the sheepish smile of Otto, Dieter and Greta's son. He'd met the kid last night and he hadn't said a word to Jesse. The lanky teenager had just stared with the same awkward smile that was across his face now. Jesse decided to break the ice. "You okay there, Otto?"

"Erm, a message... from my father," Otto managed to get out.

Jesse leaned on the doorjamb as Otto fell silent again, then lifted his eyebrows. "And what might that be?"

Otto cleared his throat. "Ya, erm. When you are ready, he... he said to meet him at his practice."

"Great," Jesse said, "and where might that be?"

"Oh," Otto said, startled. "It is next to the butcher. To the left."

"Thanks, kid. I owe you one," Jesse said and waved as he closed the door. Hearing the teen scurry away across the wooden landing, Jesse couldn't help but think about how scared he was.

The longer Jesse stayed in Bleaker's Creek, the greater the sense he was getting that this wasn't going to be as straightforward as he'd hoped. He was starting to get a bad feeling about it all. Not too strong, but definitely there, hanging around deep in his gut. Maybe he'd be better off if he just turned back for Missoula and got on a train. He could toss that little piece of paper and forget all about Lonnie.

If only it was that easy to let go of the past.

With his belly full of eggs, bacon, and some of the best coffee he'd sampled in a long time, Jesse Clayton left the inn and crossed the mud slurry of the square. He saw Red at his tent, sharpening his cleaver, bottom lip protruding again. To the left of that tent was another. This one had a wooden front, not an open flap like the butcher's, giving it a more professional look. Jesse reckoned it would probably be a tad cleaner, too.

Dieter stepped out, then stopped to hold the door for a woman and her son to walk through. He smiled at them, said something Jesse didn't catch, and they parted ways. Dieter caught sight of Jesse's approach and aimed his smile in that direction, pulling the door closed.

"Good morning, mein freund," Dieter said. Catching himself, he raised a chiding finger. "*My friend*," he swiftly corrected.

"Morning, Dieter."

"Sleep well?"

"Well enough until your kid woke me up."

"Ah! Apologies! We're all early risers here, zat is my fault! I hope it wasn't too rough on you!"

"I was more worried about Otto. He seemed awful spooked. Wondering if it's on my account."

"Ah, not at all! He'll be just fine. He was out with Kip, Red's son, hunting by themselves a few days ago and got into—how you say?—a bit of a pickle. Poor Otto has been… wary of things since. But I'm sure he'll come round soon.

Usually, he's quite the talkative one. He wants to sound like an American so bad!" Dieter snickered.

"How long have y'all been here?"

"By my count, zis will be our eighth winter."

"Then he sounds American enough to me."

"Could you do me a favor?" Dieter asked. "Could you tell him that?"

"Ain't you tried?"

"What son ever listens to his father?"

Jesse nodded slowly. While that may be true in most cases, not everyone had a father like his. There was never much choice in the matter when it came to listening. Not if you didn't want to be hurting, anyway. "Coming from somebody who didn't have quite the relationship with his daddy as Otto does," Jesse said, rubbing some feeling back into his fingers, "he might not be listening, but he's still learnin' from you all the same."

"And what did you learn from your father?"

Jesse hesitated, then picked his words carefully. "A lot of things I wish I hadn't."

"Ah," Dieter said, his tone turning morose. "I'm sorry."

"You ain't my poppa. Besides, you don't strike me as anything like him anyway." It felt strange talking about his father. It was a subject he'd not often broached after the man had died. Jesse decided he would change the subject. "So, what is it you wanted me out here for, Dieter? Or do you prefer Doc?"

"Either is fine. It's mostly Red who insists on using my title. I spend most of my time managing the inn. I seldom spend more than an hour being a doctor on any given day," Dieter said and started walking, gesturing for Jesse to follow. "I said yesterday I might know of a party with a mutual interest. It just so happens a young couple is staying here at Bleaker's. The husband—" Dieter paused and rapidly clicked his fingers. "Ah, I forget the name! No matter, he'll introduce himself, I'm sure. Where was I? Ya! The husband is looking to prospect in the area and is looking not far from where you wish to go. I had a chat wiz zem zis morning, and they were very agreeable in sharing their transport."

"You went and did that for me?"

"This is Bleaker's Creek! And you are a guest at *my* inn," Dieter said and shrugged his shoulders. "And if I am being perfectly candid, there's something in you that I cannot help but trust, mein freund."

Jesse thanked Dieter for the kind words and trust as the two of them approached a stagecoach. Smaller than the one Jesse had ridden up in with Dixie Rhodes, and a little worse for wear, too. The paintwork was chipped and faded, and the wheels were missing a spoke or two. Jesse glanced at Dieter, who raised his hands in a calming manner.

"You stare at her any harder, she may just collapse," a gruff voice said as a man stepped out from behind the stagecoach, giving Jesse an odd sense of déjà vu. Only this man wasn't Dixie Rhodes; he was taller and much broader in the chest. He also had a red beard, streaked with silver, which almost swallowed up his face underneath a fur hat. His buckskin suit was patched up in places, scuffed and muddy; the same went for his fur boots.

"Well, I'll be," Jesse said. "I ain't seen a mountain man in years."

"That's 'cause most of us don't like being seen!" the mountain man said and boomed a laugh. He introduced himself as Otis, and Jesse shook the man's big hand as he gave his name in return. "So, you looking to ride out with that couple in the coach?"

Jesse said he was.

"I'll tell you like I told them: *be careful.* And I mean *real* careful. Up there, them mountains ain't safe right now. There's plenty of animals out there looking for food before winter... and keep a mind especially of Black Fang."

"What's a Black Fang?" Jesse asked.

Otis chuckled. "You'll know him when you see him. And if you do, keep quiet and get running. He sees you? It's over." Otis turned his attention to Dieter and pulled his sack from his back. "I got something you should see, Doctor Kraus." Otis glanced at Jesse as he refrained from opening the sack.

Dieter waved his hand, dismissing Otis's distrust. "He's okay, Otis. Whatever it is, Jesse can see too."

"You said it," Otis said. He dropped the sack to the floor

and opened it up. He put his hand inside and then fished out a bloody piece of flesh. It didn't look fresh; it had a sickly sweet whiff of decay to it. Jesse could tell by the brown hair it was covered in that it was a scalp.

The doctor gasped. "Put zat away, Otis."

"Found it up on the ridge. Not much else left. No gear. No blood. Nothing. This weren't no animal. Definitely weren't the work o' Black Fang, neither," Otis said. His tone was so matter of fact, it was unsettling. That was somebody's hair he was holding. They deserved a little more respect.

Dieter put a hand on his hips and scratched at his beard. "*Scheisse*," he hissed under his breath. "I know zat hair," Dieter said, then let out a long sigh. This was the first Jesse had seen of the man under strain. He looked to be this camp's point of leadership. Jesse hadn't met the mayor or sheriff yet, that was for sure. They probably didn't even have one. Being this small and close-knit, there would be no need. A lot of people looked to Dieter around here. It would be interesting to see how he handled himself.

"What do you want me to do?" Otis asked Dieter.

"Get rid of it. There's no need to fuel any more fears around here."

"All right. Wilbur's out there laying some more traps. Should keep you all a bit more secure."

"Good. Thank you. Go and see Red. He'll have your cuttings and hides."

Otis rose back to his formidable full height. He nodded to the pair of them and then marched, bag in hand, toward the butcher. Dieter sighed again and rubbed at his temples.

"You okay there?" Jesse asked.

"Not really. I've never seen one of those up close before. And I knew whom it belonged to, as well. Poor fellow stayed here just last week. Up and vanished."

"*Huh*," Jesse said. "That the first scalp you've found?"

Dieter told him it was.

"And just how many people exactly have you had go missing since your mystery man Indian started showing up?"

"Half a dozen, at least that we know of."

"Huh," Jesse said again, hands on hips.

Dieter adjusted his glasses and straightened himself. "You find zat... amusing?" Dieter asked, irritation barbing his tone.

"Not amusing, just interesting. Never seen Cheyenne or Navajo work like that, is all."

"Maybe zey are not Cheyenne or Navajo."

Jesse watched the trees as he thought about the scalp. How it didn't quite fit, somehow. It just felt a little... off to him. How, though, he couldn't quite put his finger on. "True. Not sure how tribes operate around here, I guess."

"No. You don't," Dieter said. "Come now, let me introduce you to Clarence and Joan. And then you can be on your way. Very carefully, might I add."

It wasn't long before they got to traveling. Jesse had met the young couple he was now riding with.

Joan was quiet but smiled plenty. Long, chestnut hair pulled back in a bun, she wore pants and boots, with a thick coat to keep her warm. He'd half expected her to be wearing a dress.

Clarence was dressed for the trip. In boots and a duster, iron on his hip. He had the boyish look of a young man who'd only ever carried a gun. Jesse would bet that he'd fired it at nothing that could shoot back. Should things go south, Jesse wasn't sure he could be counted on. Not that he thought things would. The road was well-trodden. As long as the wagon held out, he didn't see the need for them to find trouble.

While they were inside the stagecoach, up top, their driver braved the rushing cold. His name was Jed. Bald, and with fewer teeth than he had fingers on his left hand, he hadn't been much for talking at all. Jesse had just left him to it, deciding to ride in the relative warmth of the coach instead of riding shotgun.

"...And that's the plan, really," Clarence had been detailing his plan for prospecting the mountains. He had done so on and off for the past few hours. "Stake out a few good plots here to start with. I'll find what I believe to be the most prosperous locations, then bring back a larger force in the late spring. Then we'll start digging around!"

The thrum and rumbling of the running wheels reverberating through the wooden seat soothed Jesse as they rode on. "Sounds good," Jesse said, for the sake of manners. At least the young man had the enthusiasm. He'd need it. Prospectors Jesse had known were miserable. One had called it a 'perk of the job,' due to a long career of finding exactly nothing.

"What makes you so sure there's gold out here, Clarence? Plenty of places have turned up nothin' but fools in the past decade. Fewer claims every year," Jesse said.

Clarence tapped his nose. "I know that, sir. But they're all still looking down in Cal-ee-fornya. Not me. No sir. I'm looking up here. And you know why it's such a good idea?" Clarence was grinning as he finished his sentence.

"I could probably guess," Jesse said.

"Then do so kindly, Mr. Clayton."

Jesse leaned forward. "Because nobody else is."

Clarence slapped his knee. "You're *goddamn* right!" The young man almost jumped up out of his seat. Shame, Jesse thought, it may have been funny to see him hit his head. Might have even knocked some sense into the kid. He had balls, though, Jesse would give him that much. "Are you sure I can't tempt you in on this venture with us, Mr. Clayton? An extra set of hands would speed things up mightily!

"What the hell do they need soothing for?" Clarence moaned.

A boom came from the trees. Red erupted from Clarence's chest. He wheezed as he fell to his knees, and then face-first into the mud. Jesse snatched his gun and fanned off two shots as he strafed to the cover of the wagon. Jed started moving, clambering up to his seat. Jesse peeled from the cover, keeping the horses between himself and the tree line. Jed, shotgun in hand, looked down at the barrel Jesse now pointed at him.

"Steady now, Clayton," Jed said.

"You in on this, Jed?"

"A man's gotta make a livin'," Jed said. "Put down the gun, and I can see to it you'll live."

Jesse pulled the trigger. The driver pinwheeled backward off the stagecoach and into the dirt. Back pressed against the wagon again, Jesse opened the loading gate on his Colt and thumbed in fresh rounds.

"Come on out, now," called a deep and familiar voice.

Jesse stepped out from the wagon and the horses with his pistol raised. Otis stood in the road, arms clasped around the long frame of a Hawken rifle. Not aiming to shoot, Otis seemed relaxed for a man who had just murdered another in cold blood.

"Put that away, fool. You ain't getting out of here."

"That so?" Jesse said.

"Look around you, son. Where are you gonna go? Go

on. Run. This land ain't yours. It'll just kill ya slower than I will."

Jesse thumbed back the hammer. "Not if I put a bullet in you, Otis. I don't often miss from this range."

"Oh, come on now, you're already beat. Think about it."

Otis's overconfidence was bugging him, and again something didn't feel right. Jesse sure as hell didn't feel like he was holding the winning hand at that moment. He was missing something. He thought back to their conversation earlier in the morning with Dieter. Holding the scalp, Otis had said something about... *Wilbur,* his partner.

Oh, hell.

Jesse stepped back just as the huge round punched the mud where his foot had been a second before. Globs of muck sprayed up and Jesse shielded his eyes. In flinching from the round, Jesse's aim had faltered away from Otis. By the time he realized and wrestled for control of his reflexes, he saw that Otis had drawn a pistol of his own.

The gun roared.

Jesse's head snapped back with a spray of blood. He stumbled backward and his bloodied Stetson hit the ground. Jesse's boot found only air where he thought the ground should have been.

INTERLUDE ONE

He watched everything unfold from the shadows of the trees.

He had looked on, silent and still, as the man in the hat had gunned down his friend, only to be then shot himself and plummet over the edge of the rise. He had tumbled and skidded down the steep muddy slope. Surely dead.

Maybe the dead man would have something of use.

The man who had emerged from the trees shouted and another walked out to meet him. This one looked much older and smaller, stepping slowly in a poncho that drowned his frame. The two of them met on the road and spoke. The distance was too far and their dialogue too quiet for anything to be heard.

The bigger of the mountain men walked to the edge

and looked down. Then he picked up the dead man's hat and turned it in his hand, examining it like some creature he had for the first time this day laid eyes on. Taking the hat with him, he approached the stagecoach. The two mountain men spoke again, and then the older one clambered up onto the top of the coach and took the reins of the horses. The bigger one opened the door. He stood for a moment, talking to somebody inside. Even from here, the predatory grin on the mountain man's face was visible. The face of a beast about to toy with its prey. The man took one last glance around before squeezing his big frame inside the coach.

A woman's scream rang out.

The older one snapped the reins and the horses began to pull the stagecoach up the road.

He turned away, walking back into the trees as the woman's cries continued. There was nothing else for him here, for now at least. Instead, he would make his way down into the forest below. He chose his steps, avoiding anything that could betray him with sound. Silence was the key to navigating the forest. He would be nothing more than a leaf carried on the wind. He would visit the dead man and see what use could be made of him.

If the wolves did not reach him first.

4

PHANTOM BROTHER

Wake up, Jesse. Come on now, get up!

Jesse opened his eyes. Hearing Jonah's voice, he expected to see his brother. But he wasn't there. instead, seeing nothing but thick clouds smeared across the sky, he wondered if he was staring at heaven. He was soon convinced otherwise when he felt the searing pain in his head.

It all came rushing back to him: The two mountain men who'd ambushed them, the shot that almost took his foot, then the other that had almost taken his head. A tenth of an inch lower and he wouldn't be thinking how goddamn lucky he was right now. He tried to lift his arm to check the damage.

It wouldn't budge.

Jesse looked down at himself. He was half sunk in the

mud. He must have been tumbling at some speed to get this stuck; again, it appeared Jesse had had another stroke of luck. Harder ground may have left him broken in several places.

Jesse started to flex and wiggle his stuck limbs. Underneath the ground, he could feel them starting to get more and more room as his limbs wore away at the thick, mulchy earth. His left hand came free first. He shook off the mud and then used it to help pry out his other arm. He worked his legs, pumping them up and down, steadily feeling the greater range in them as the mud writhed and rippled in front of him.

Something hissed to his right.

Jesse's head turned to the sound, and he froze. A long, thick, ropey body coiled around a tree, slithering its way down to the base. Its head bobbed left and right as it slalomed its way toward Jesse. A light brown body lined with dark stripes, its four feet in length ended in the hard keratin rings of a rattle. Jesse knew one thing in particular about Prairie Rattlesnakes: they were the only snake in this part of the frontier known for their bite to have aftereffect.

It was moving toward him, drawn by the struggling movements and his body heat. It likely thought he was smaller, being trapped in the mud. He had a choice to make. It wasn't rising on itself, and he had yet to hear that telltale rattle of warning just yet, so it might just slither on by him when it saw him to be too big of a meal. He could just wait.

His other option was to keep struggling until he could free his boot, grab the knife he had tucked in there and see who was quicker on the draw. He couldn't use his gun; he'd lost that somewhere in the fall. No, this would all come down to a matter of fangs or blade.

The hissing Prairie inched closer. Jesse kept his eyes on the reptile as he started to wiggle his left leg again. The toe of his boot poked free of the mud. The rattler stopped. The boot kept pushing through the mud and the rattler's head started to rise along with it. The Prairie's tail started to shake, emitting a coarse rasp that made Jesse forget about the pain in his head and freeze. The snake was no more than a foot away. Easily close enough to strike at his arm.

Their bite wasn't necessarily fatal for a grown man, but Jesse wasn't exactly feeling in tip-top condition. And not knowing where in the hell he was, he could do without trying to contend with the pain, the swelling, and the bleeding. He'd also heard of much more adverse effects of a Prairie bite, too: fever, delirium, and even paralysis. He couldn't risk it.

Jesse lowered his boot slowly back into the mud. The rattling died down but the snake still kept its head raised, watching the potential threat of Jesse's boot go back into its hiding hole. Satisfied Jesse's footwear was no longer a threat, the snake lowered its head again. Its forked tongue sampled the air, then it began to move forward again, right toward Jesse's chest.

He took a deep breath and held it.

The rattlesnake slithered onto his shoulder and across his chest. Jesse felt its surprising weight on him and the cool scales as it undulated its way over him. He watched its tongue protrude and the black abyss of its eye. Could it see him? Could it sense his pounding heart in his chest? His diaphragm was starting to spasm. The rattle passed him as the snake slithered off of Jesse. He let out a long, slow breath, careful to do it as quietly as possible. He waited for the snake to get some distance away, then worked his legs free.

Jesse stood up and felt the world spin. His vision blurred and he reached out for the tree to keep himself steady. He took a few deep breaths and waited for his heart to stop pounding against his ribs.

Two brushes with death today. Why did he have the feeling they wouldn't be the only ones?

Feeling steadier on his feet, he found a stream nearby and washed the mud from his hands. His clothes were caked in it, but at least it would help keep him warm. In the reflection of the water, he looked at his head and saw where the bullet had caught him.

A torrent of blood had run down his left cheek from his hairline. The bullet had just glanced the top of his head, parting his hair and his skin, leaving a bloody mess of matted hair. It looked ugly and it throbbed like the worst case of barrel fever Jesse had ever had. But he didn't see any bone or brain, so he thanked his lucky stars and splashed the wound with water. He cursed at the cold water's sting on his raw skin. But he needed to at least try and get it as clean as he could.

Jesse had learned about infection a couple of years back from a doctor who had treated a cut he'd suffered when bringing in a bounty with Sarah. He'd talked about how important it was to keep wounds clean, preferably with alcohol or boiled water. *But at the very least keep dirt out of it and don't go poking at it, goddamn it!* he'd said. Jesse couldn't recall the doctor's name, but that wound had healed up quicker than any other he'd had. And with little scarring, too.

If the doctor was right, his mud-covered wounds out here could be just as fatal as that Prairie Rattler's bite. Jesse checked himself over and found a few minor injuries, nothing to be a matter of concern for now; just a few scratches on his arms, a cut on his left hand, and bangs that would soon bruise.

His left hand was cut deep enough to bleed, so he tore off a piece of his shirt that was almost clean and wrapped a makeshift bandage, tying off the knot using his right hand and his teeth. His pants were torn up a little, as was his coat. He could always get new ones, and for that he was grateful; it was mighty harder trying to replace limbs.

Jesse surveyed his surroundings and thought about his best course of action. He had the day with him, it not being much past noon. Time was on his side, which was good, but even with that in mind, he wasn't sure if he would be able to find his way to somewhere safe before nightfall. He didn't think much of his chances of getting through the night, either. The stream he was next to would lead to the river, which he could follow to either a road or a settlement. Jesse might even get lucky and wind up back at Bleaker's Creek. But how long was the stream? Might could be it was too much of a detour to get him back safely in time.

"Come on, Jess."

"Don't call me tha—" Jesse had snapped the words almost as a reflex, without thinking. He'd stopped midsentence when he saw who was speaking. Atop of a rock just downstream, dressed just like he used to be in his brown pants with the blue patches sewn over the knees, sat a young boy that looked a lot like Jesse. A nest of thick, haylike brown hair, with strands of red (a gift from his mother) topped a thin, grubby face that housed icy-blue eyes, and a smile that filled Jesse with a familiar sense of safety. "*Jonah*? Jonah is that you?"

"Little brother, who else am I gon' be? Santa Claus?" Jonah inspected fingernails that were clogged with dirt. "He ain't gon' be the one look out for you, is he?"

Jesse's vision swirled and a sense of dizziness struck him. He dropped to a knee and rubbed at his eyes. He looked up again and his brother was gone. Jesse stood up and sighed heavily. Maybe this gunshot to the head had knocked a few brain cells loose. His brother didn't look like that anymore for two reasons: the first being that he wasn't that young; the second being that Jonah Clayton was dead. Had been for ten years, now.

"Do I look dead to you, little brother?" Jonah said, beside him now.

Jesse jumped back, startled. "Christ, Jonah!"

"He won't help ya, nothin'. But I will. Listen here, Jess. What you need to do is find yourself some high ground. See if there ain't nothin' you recognize to find your way. Just like Poppa went and taught us."

"Sure," Jesse said, eyeing his phantom brother suspiciously. The kid-but-older-brother was talking a whole heap of sense. "Where'd be best, you think?"

Jonah's scrawny teenage face screwed up as he looked around, concentrating, as he figured out the best place. "There, I reckon," he said, poking a filthy finger over Jesse's shoulder.

Jesse turned. A high hill, not too difficult to climb from the looks of it, either. It looked like a good bet. Jesse turned back to his brother. "You know, that doesn't look half—"

Jonah was gone.

Jesse looked all around, but his brother had vanished. No, he corrected himself, his brother had never been there. It was all just a hallucination brought on by the bullet to his head. Hopefully, that and the dizziness would be the worst of the side effects.

Jesse cast one last look up to where he had fallen from—and what a height it had been—then looked down at where he had ended up. A few yards from where he'd crashed into the dirt, something caught his eye, glinting in the noon sunlight. He wandered over to it. He clawed at the mud and then pulled it free: his Colt Single Action Army.

Well, looks like my luck hasn't quite run dry yet.

As if in answer, Jesse heard the distant howl of a wolf, quickly joined by more. Fate was quick to tip the scales back into balance today, it seemed. Jesse gave the gun a quick wash in the stream and then holstered it. He glanced around again, trying to place where the howls had emanated from, then started for the hill that his ethereal brother had suggested.

∽

THE WOLVES HOWLED AGAIN. They sounded much closer this time, too. Jesse had gotten about halfway up the rise, occasionally stopping to rest against a tree or getting snagged on a bush. He felt stiff and sluggish as he moved, slowed down by pain and drying mud, but he knew stopping for too long a rest would ultimately do more harm than good.

As he'd listened and watched for the wolves, he'd heard

something faintly across to the east. Following the sound, he eventually caught sight of the river below him. Relief bloomed in his chest, and he couldn't help but smile. He'd been closer to the river than expected. Jesse thought he might make it to Bleaker's Creek before nightfall after all.

Descending the hill toward it, passing trees he once knew the names of, he kept thinking about how he used to spend his days running through the forest with Jonah. They'd lived in a small cabin down South. The two of them, along with their mother and father. They'd explored that forest a lot as kids, skimming rocks off the streams, hand fishing for trout and bass, and stumbling across all sorts of animals they had no business with.

All that changed when Poppa had come back from the War. For Jesse, that was the only Poppa he could remember. Fun exploration had stopped. Instead, it was learning to track and to hunt: how to survive. There wasn't any fun in the way Poppa had taught it, either. Put a foot wrong and he was likely to strike you like a viper. If they were lucky, it'd be a tongue-lashing. If not so lucky, it was his hand. He remembered Jonah getting a lot of it, sometimes sparing Jesse from it.

Jesse spotted a garter snake weaving through the grass. The bright orange stripes on its neck gave it away. That was a good sign. Snakes tended to roam near riverbeds as they were great hunting grounds for prey seeking a drink. He knew he wasn't too far away from the river now and pushed on a little faster, still having a mind not to stir up too much noise. Those wolves were around, and who knew what else could be, too.

Black Fang, maybe.

The ground started to flatten out and the trees started to thin, too. But with this upturn in fortune, Jesse saw the counterbalance of fate.

Snared by the ankle, suspended about ten feet from the ground by a rope, a deer hung lifelessly still. It hadn't been there long enough to starve, but something big had happened across it and made a meal of it, it seemed. Blood splattered the grass and trees around it, while its belly had been opened up, entrails and viscera dangling beside it. A dozen flies busied themselves around it too, buzzing with delight. Jesse also noted the huge scratches on the tree nearby. This had been the work of a grizzly.

But the mountain men had set the trap.

How many did they have out here? And was it just these snares to be on the watch for? Jesse's head started to ache anew as he had this new threat to contend with. Not only did he have to fare against nature, but he also had his fellow man to contend with. It was going to be a long day. Jesse hoped it wouldn't stretch into another one.

He moved past the hanging corpse and moved on, slowing right down now; he had to be vigilant for traps. The mountain men clearly had a wide reach when it came to the territory around Bleaker's Creek. Snares were one thing, but Jesse had an idea that the two of them would not be against the idea of deadlier ploys. The deer had been there longer than a few days, so these traps probably weren't checked regularly. Which meant their deployment was for more nefarious means than survival.

What did Otis and Wilbur have to gain from setting up so many traps, causing unnecessary deaths like that of this poor animal? Maybe there was something out here that they were afraid of. Maybe they weren't responsible for all the disappearances around Bleaker's Creek. Maybe it was—

A shadow crossed a tree to his right. Jesse glimpsed it in his peripheral vision. Turning his attention to the shade of the dense thicket, he hoped it was just his eyes playing tricks on him. The leaves on a bush nearby moved as if they had just been displaced. Jesse kept still and watched it.

Nothing.

Jesse moved on, and the sound of the rushing water ahead was growing louder now. A bout of dizziness struck him; his vision started to swirl and swim, and he stumbled, falling against a tree. He leaned against it, trying to blink away the waves in his eyes, waiting for whoever it was that borrowed his legs to give them back.

Come on Clayton. Breathe it out. Just breathe. It'll pass.

He raised his head, and all seemed right again. No blurry view, and nobody seemingly trying to pull the world out from underneath him. He tentatively touched the wound on his head. It was damned sore and hot to the touch. His fingers came away with thick, blotchy blood on them. He figured that was a good sign: the bleeding was slowing down. He'd worry about ugly scabs and scars and ruined hair later.

The bush to his right rustled again. And so did the one next to it. Around him, Jesse could sense movement. Multiple forms darted between the shadows and the cover of foliage. Almost silent, if not for the snitching whispers of leaves. Jesse knew then that something was tracking him. He was being followed.

No, Jesse Clayton was being *hunted*.

He was outnumbered. What he wasn't sure of was how many there were. He realized he hadn't heard the wolves in a while and guessed that answered the question as to what he was being tracked by. He wouldn't be able to outrun them. He wasn't even sure he could run all that well in the first place. He could fire off a round and hope it scattered them, but he couldn't guarantee it would work. Besides, how long would it keep them away? He didn't have a whole lot of rounds. Plus, that sound might draw the attention of something else. Something bigger.

The river!

Of course! If he could get to the river, he would be safe. He could dive in if he needed to and let the current carry him on to safety. That was if it wasn't too strong. Still, Jesse fancied his chances with a few rough rapids a lot more than he did with a pack of ravenous wolves.

Jesse drew his Colt. He started side-stepping, constantly glancing forward to keep an eye out for any traps, and back for any unwanted visitors looking to get the jump on him. He kept going, not seeing movement or traps. His pulse throbbed in his neck. He no longer felt the cold. A hundred yards or so, that was it.

Oh, hell.

Two shapes had moved through the trees to move ahead of him. The wolves were moving to cut him off. He couldn't carry on at this pace or he'd end up surrounded. He turned and ran, pounding the dirt with his boots and pumping his arms. The trees were opening up the way for him, and he could see the river in the distance.

Behind him, his hunters had abandoned their cautious approach. He could hear their skittering claws clatter the ground in pursuit. It sounded like a lot of them. A lot more than he could shoot. Jesse pushed faster on his protesting legs. A needle was starting to slide its way underneath his kneecap, every step tapping it further in. Jesse gritted his teeth against the pain. Wolf bites would be a lot more painful than that, he reminded himself and pressed his legs that little bit harder. He could hear their labored pants behind him now. He could imagine their lolling tongues dripping saliva in their wake, their hungry eyes focused solely on him.

He'd halved the distance now. The noise of the river was a welcoming roar, enticing him and his tiring legs. His head pounded, his lungs burned and—

Something snagged his right ankle.

Suddenly, Jesse was pulled off his feet. He hit the ground and his Colt clattered away from him. He felt his hip clunk as he was jerked up and into the air, rising up and into the canopy, finally halting ten feet from the ground. He hung there, dazed, with his arms dangling. Helpless.

The wolves closed in on their strung-up dinner.

Jesse shook away the daze and saw his world upside down. He was looking up at a pack of eight wolves hanging from a grassy ceiling. Panting and prowling, they slowly circled him. He saw one of them pass over his gun. A wolf jumped up and Jesse had to pull his arms away from its snapping jaw.

"Goddamn mountain men," Jesse said as he swayed in the air. He needed to figure out a way of getting rid of these wolves quickly. He could feel the blood rushing to his head already, and the pressure on his bullet wound was already tipping toward unbearable. He had minutes before it would put him unconscious. Then he'd be as good as dead.

What Jesse needed was a nice, big, loud noise. Scary enough to scatter these hungry mutts just long enough for him to cut himself down. If only he hadn't dropped his damned gun, he chided himself. Jesse looked around, thinking like a fool there'd be something he could use.

The wolves all froze. Their ears pricked up in unison. Jesse found that odd.

Then he heard a long, deep, billowing roar in the distance. Loud and savage enough for Jesse to feel it reverberate in his bones and send an awful chill down his spine. The wolves whined and scattered in all directions, leaving Jesse alone.

He wasted no time, bringing his knee up and reaching for the knife in his boot, before straining his every muscle to reach the rope that had snared his right boot. There was another leviathan roar as Jesse sawed through the rope and he felt another chill run from the base of his neck right down his spine. He didn't even feel it as his ass hit the ground.

He picked himself up, retrieved his dropped Colt, and ran for the river.

He wanted to be as far away from whatever was making that noise as possible.

5

BLACK FANG

The river was there all right. It was just fifty feet below him. The current rushed by, breaking on huge rocks strewn along the river. It would be a little more than a rough ride. Jesse thought about just jumping, but the risk of catching the stony crevasse on his way down was risky. If he made it into the water, he could then hit one of those big rocks as he tried to right himself in the current's pull.

Jesse glanced back into the trees. Thankfully, there were no signs of the wolves or of whatever had made those monstrous roars. He started walking, and the hillside started to decline, taking him closer to the bed. Should he need to, riding the river would be a much safer task.

"That's not a bad idea, little brother," Jonah said.

Jesse started to see his phantom older brother walking beside him again. "You can't keep doing that, Jonah."

"Sure, I can," Jonah said, "That's my job. Keep you on your toes, so you don't end up eaten."

"You can do that without scarin' me half dead, you know."

Jonah smiled, showing off his dimpled cheeks. "But where would the fun in that be?"

Jesse shrugged. "I know you're just in my head, but hell if you don't sound just like him."

"You knew me better than anyone else did. Even Momma."

"What about Demi Barrett?" Jesse asked, watching for his brother's reaction.

Jonah shoved his hands in his pockets. It was his turn to shrug. "She knew me in ways you didn't, sure. But she never knew the *real* me. You did."

Jesse wasn't expecting that. He'd never heard his brother talk like that about Demi. Maybe that bullet had done a little more damage than he'd first thought. "So, what should I be doing next, Jonah?" Jesse asked, deciding to change the subject instead of dwelling on a past he'd rather stay behind, and knowing full well he was talking to himself.

"Keep doin' what you're doin'. Followin' the river is the best thing to do. You're bound to find some folks eventually."

"What if they ain't the friendly kind?"

Jonah answered with another question. "You still got your gun don't you?"

Jesse opened his mouth to answer and stopped himself. His gaze had wandered across the river and up the mountain. He wasn't sure how he'd spotted him, but somehow he'd known exactly where to look. Across the way and watching him again, just like he had on the ride to Bleaker's Creek in Dixie Rhodes' wagon, was the Indian. The man was so still, it could have been as if he was cut from stone.

"Who the hell is *that*?" Jonah said.

"Your guess is as good as mine."

"You've seen him before?" Jonah asked.

"He was a lot farther away the last time."

"So he's followin' you?"

"Might could be. Quite the coincidence if he ain't."

"You should give him a wave," Jonah said.

Jesse turned to him with a condescending frown. "And why would I do that, exactly?"

"Well, it ain't like he's gon' see me do it, is he?" Jonah said, hands on hips. "You gotta—I dunno—let him know you're friendly."

"Because that'll make him think twice about killing me, huh?"

"He's probably gonna kill ya anyway, Jess. Doesn't hurt to try."

Jesse let out a long sigh. "Fine." No wonder people who

talked to themselves were damned crazy. They probably had to put up with crap like this from their long-dead siblings constantly. "If I give him a wave, will you shut up?"

"Sure," Jonah said with another dimpled smile.

Jesse turned back to the stranger, still locked in place across the river. Tentatively, Jesse raised his hand and sheepishly waved.

"Come on, give it a bit more than *that*," Jonah said.

Jesse wiped the air in front of him with great swings of his arm. The stranger did nothing.

"Happy now?" Jesse asked, turning to his brother.

Jonah was gone. *At least he was true to his word*, Jesse thought and looked back across the river.

The stranger was gone too.

~

Getting to the riverbed wasn't going to be as easy as he'd thought. He could see it all right; Jesse would just need to climb twenty feet down a rock face. He stretched out his arms and his legs, feeling the strain and the tightness in his muscles. The bruises and strains from his run-in with Bradshaw's gang on the train still weren't healed. Now, with the added scrapes from his tumble down the mountain, he was feeling pretty stiff.

He sat on the edge and then gingerly started to turn and lower himself down, dangling a boot until he found purchase on a jutting rock. It was slow going, but he carefully started to descend the rock wall, digging his hands into gaps and toeing his boots onto ledges and into grooves. Vines and ivy clinging to the rocks didn't help. Jesse almost lost his footing and his grip once or twice on the slippery plants.

His vision startled to ripple, and his stomach somersaulted. He felt himself pull away from the rock and pressed himself into it, seizing his fingers around whatever it was he was holding. Jesse squeezed his eyes shut and started to breathe through the dizziness. He counted to ten on long inhales through his nose, and to ten again as he blew out of his mouth.

Get a hold of yourself, Clayton.

The giddiness passed. Jesse opened his eyes. A spider dangled from a strand of web inches from his face. Thin legs worked the thread from its bulbous abdomen. The tiny arachnid was no bigger than his fingertip. Fascinated, he watched its spinnerets work together like knitting needles to make the sticky string, and then his eyes were drawn to the stark red of the little shape above it. Jesse thought it looked like an hourglass; he mused at how bright it was.

He turned his attention back to climbing, leaving the spider be. Ignoring it, he found fresh footings and clambered down the mountain. He'd descended about another foot when he felt a tickle on his left hand. Jesse looked up.

The hourglass spider was back. *Would you look at that,*

Jesse thought, *I've gone and made myself a friend*. The spider's legs were delicate on Jesse's skin, and with each step, he felt the softest tickling sweep of its legs. It was a touch too much. He shook his hand gently to coax the spider off. It wouldn't move.

"Come on now, little buddy, off you get. Unlike you, my arms are getting tired 'cause I can't stick to walls," Jesse said. He thought the spider was almost regarding him, its eight, tiny black eyes glinting in the afternoon sun. Jesse shook his hand again, a little more emphatically this time. The little spider still would not move. He shook it again, three great whips of his wrist. The damned thing was still there.

The spider darted forward. It made a beeline for the sleeve of his coat. The tickling sensation was unbearable as it crossed the fine hairs on his wrist.

"Oh, no, you don't!" Jesse said and shook his whole arm violently, bracing himself to the rock with the rest of his body. He bashed it too, hoping the collision would dislodge the spider. He could still feel the intolerable tingle of the spider's legs. It was close to his cuff now.

Jesse drew in a lungful of air and brought his wrist up to his face. He pursed his lips as if to whistle, but forcefully exhaled instead. The spider flew off in a gust of air and spittle. Jesse then rubbed the back of his hand on the stubble of his chin, grateful for its scratchiness to relieve his itchy hand.

Jesse climbed the rest of the way down the damp rocks without instance, dropping the last five feet, thinking he could probably survive a fall like that, even in his condition. He stood for a moment, letting the pulsing fire in his ribs abate and thinking how the tiniest spider he'd ever seen just almost killed him. If he'd slipped, who knew what could have happened?

"Damn right, that thing could have killed you."

Jesse flinched and resisted the urge to reach for his gun. "Damn it, Jonah! Would you *stop*?"

"What? It's not like I can warn you or nothin'," Jonah said. He leaned against a tree to Jesse's left, chewing on a twig.

His brother had a point. "Okay, then. Maybe next time wave or something first. Don't just appear and start talkin'. Already nearly got killed by a spider just now. I don't need a ghost finishing the job."

"Yep. Real lucky there with that little critter. If he'd a bit you..." Jonah finished his sentence with a long and low whistle.

"What're you talkin' about? You sayin' that little thing up there tryin' to tickle me to death was poisonous?"

"Not poisonous, no. *Venomous*," Jonah said, emphasizing that last fancy word. Jesse raised an eyebrow at his brother and frowned. Jonah was either trying to be funny, or there was more to come. He waited. "Poisonous is stuff you *eat*. Venomous is things that *bite*," Jonah added.

"Well, I am over head and ears in awe of your knowledge there, brother."

Jonah took the stick out of his mouth and pointed it at Jesse, the end all marked and mushy from where he'd been chewing. "You don't believe me?"

"Of course not. I ain't never seen a spider that small be so dangerous. And neither have you. Or is it a special thing being a ghost, you being all full of wisdom now?" Jesse said. He tried to sell his best-sounding condescending voice, but it was a little startling at just how deep these conversations were with his brother. Sure, he'd known him for years, but there were likely lots of things he had forgotten about his brother: conversations, fights, and arguments they'd had as kids. That was a lot for his mind to play with. But why conjure up Jonah for a conversation over a spider? Why not flash up some old memories? Jesse didn't understand, and trying to was starting to bring on the beginnings of another headache.

Deciding to drop the issue, Jesse started walking to the river bed. The trees were sparse and the grass gave way to hardened dirt which, as he got closer to the river, became a bank of stones, pebbles, and rocks. Jesse found the din of the rushing waves soothing, and the air around a river always felt that little bit fresher and crisp.

"I ain't here to talk to you about the spider, Jess," said Jonah, who was walking along with him now. He decided he was done with his stick and so he tossed it into the river.

Jesse watched it arc through the air and then into the river. It made no splash. That made his head hurt, too.

"So, you weren't there to save me from the tiny spider with the death bite?" Jesse said with a smirk.

"You don't wanna believe me, that's fine, brother. But like I said, that's not why I'm here."

"Come on then, spill."

"I'm here to warn you about *that*," Jonah said, pointing. Jesse followed the tip of his finger to where he was indicating and saw a tree adorned with an all-too-familiar sight. Deep, long gouges marked the tree. The kind of scratches done with thick and powerful claws. He'd seen those kinds of markings enough times to know what it was that had made them.

Jesse swallowed. Hard. "Well, aren't you just my little guardian angel," Jesse said to his brother. Alas, the Phantom Clayton had once again disappeared.

Claw marks on a tree weren't necessarily a bad thing. Bears clawed trees as a means to mark their territory. That was what Poppa had said when Jesse was a kid. He'd also been the one to say that seeing them wasn't necessarily a bad thing either, as they were just warnings to other bears. If you were seeing a marked tree, you were likely at the edge of said bear's territory. A place where the bear would likely *not* be.

What worried Jesse was the size. He approached the tree and inspected the deep gashes in the bark. Inches across, they were the biggest claw marks in a tree he'd ever seen... and by a considerable margin too. They were jagged and messy, with an erratic, feral, and almost unhinged quality to them. Jesse ran his hand across them and felt the ragged and coarse wounds of the tree.

Oh, they're there all right. It ain't your eyes fooling you, Clayton.

Jesse would keep quiet and move fast through here. There was always the escape route of the river should the worst happen. He moved on along the riverbed, keeping just inside the tree line for the shade and dirt, keeping a mind of just how much noise he was making. Jesse didn't want to go and make himself a target now. He was sure to keep his eyes peeled for snares, and for that matter, any other kind of trap Jesse could think of.

Over the din of the water, Jesse heard something. Or, to be more accurate, he no longer heard something. How long had the birds around him not been chirping and singing their songs? Things had become a lot quieter around him, and that did nothing but fill Jesse Clayton with dread.

There were precisely two reasons why birds would stop singing. The first one was pretty straightforward: because they were sleeping. As far as Jesse was aware, the kind of bird that liked to make noise wasn't nocturnal. The second reason, and the probable one for right now: a predator was nearby.

As Jesse continued, a low, thumping sound gradually

became louder and louder. Jesse got a few more steps before he stopped completely. He froze in place as an icy hand seized his heart and his mouth ran dry. He fought the urge to swallow, for fear of its sound giving him away.

Oh, hell.

There it was. Pitching its huge paws into an unfortunate oak tree about a hundred yards away, pulling away chips of its bark, was undoubtedly the biggest grizzly Jesse had ever seen. Upright on its chunky hind legs, it wasn't even standing up straight and Jesse could see it was comfortably over seven feet in height. A thick, muscular hump stood out above its shoulder blades—the telltale sign of a grizzly, so Poppa had told him. Its body was covered in thick hazelnut brown fur... and blood coated its forepaws.

Jesse needed a plan. And fast. He drew his Colt and checked how many rounds were in the cylinder. Satisfied, he thumbed back the trigger and raised the gun high above his head.

Let's see how you like loud noises, you big son of a gun.

The booming report of the Colt rang out across the river, bouncing through the hills. The bear stopped what it was doing and turned its big head toward Jesse. Dried blood flecked the fur around its mouth and a large black nose twitched and puckered at a new scent in the air. The bear turned its whole body to Jesse now and dropped down to all fours.

Why are you not running away?

Jesse lowered his gun and now trained it on the bear. The huge beast bared its teeth. Teeth as long as fingers lined its mouth, but Jesse was drawn to one in particular. Its left fang was broken at the tip and the tooth had turned a sickly grey. The gum around it had become black. Now Jesse understood what the people of Bleaker's Creak had been referring to when they said the name Black Fang.

The bear charged at Jesse, powering itself forward on its thick legs. Jesse squeezed the trigger on his Colt. The round struck the bear in the shoulder, and it kept coming with barely a flinch. Jesse fired two more times to the same effect.

He dove out of the charging bear's path just as it lunged forward. Black Fang crashed into a tree while Jesse scrambled along the ground and onto his feet. It reared up again and let out another roar, this one even more furious and deranged than the last.

Jesse ran, side-stepping trees and leaping bushes as he headed for the river. This was a fight he had no chance of winning, so he'd try his luck with the rapids. He could hear the bear's pounding paws clambering behind him. Black Fang's huge talons chewed up the ground and the distance between them.

Jesse vaulted a boulder, wincing at the pain in his ribs but breathing through it. *Not far to go now,* he thought, his boots pounding across the pebbles of the bed. A few seconds later, he could hear the splashing scrapes of Black

Fang, as it too reached the bed. Its claws flung up stones in its pursuit of Jesse.

Jesse took three long steps through the deepening water before leaping into a dive. The icy water sought to steal his breath as he hit the river, but he held his nerve against the cold shock and pumped his arms and kicked his legs as fast as he could, aiming to get depth and distance between him and Black Fang.

Jesse broke the surface and gasped for air. He settled himself, treading water beneath him, and wiped the hair from his face. He floated as the current carried him at a steady pace and glanced around, looking for Black Fang. He locked eyes with the bear, which had thankfully decided not to pursue him into the water. It watched him, mouth agape with its unsightly dead tooth on display.

Jesse punched the air. "Woo!" he yelled, his shout bouncing back at him from the banks. He decided he'd let the current carry him for a while. Only, he noted that the speed of it was picking up, and quite considerably at that. Jesse turned in the water and saw why.

Two hundred yards downriver... it ended.

"Oh, hell!" he shouted over the growing roar of the rapids. He tried to start swimming, but he knew he had no chance of reaching either bank of the river in time. He tried to find purchase on a passing boulder in the water, but his soaking fingers slipped right off of it, and Jesse bounced downstream. He bounced off two more before realizing he'd need an alternative plan.

He spied an overhanging branch. Jesse paddled as hard as he could to get within reach of it before he was swept past. As he approached, he shot up a hand and grabbed hold of the dangling branch. He jerked as his momentum was halted, only for the feeble arm of the tree to snap under the force. The river embraced Jesse again and pulled him to the mouth of the waterfall.

Seconds away from plummeting to his likely death, Jesse glanced around desperately in one last-ditch effort.

He saw nothing.

Jesse started to take long and deep breaths and made his body as straight as he could, imagining himself to be a blade. He took one last deep breath, held it, then closed his eyes.

Jesse felt the hands of gravity as he was yanked down the cascade.

INTERLUDE TWO

The dead man was alive after all.

Quite the amazing thing, not only to cheat death from a bullet to the head but also a fall such as that.

All the stars and all the Gods must have been watching over him this day.

The dead man had gathered himself, evaded a rattlesnake, and then ventured his way through the forest. He was rather amusing to watch. The dead man was strange in his ways, talking to people who were not there. Clumsily, he avoided those hunters' traps and narrowly escaped the wolves when he finally did trip one.

Maybe it was not the Gods favoring him. The dead man had defied death once; maybe he had a knack for survival.

The Indian watched as the dead man went on and had

his encounter with the bear. So close to the time of the Great Slumber for them, their hunger made them insatiable and incredibly ferocious at this time of year. And yet again, the Indian had watched as the dead man evaded the bear.

He had also watched as the river's strength proved too much for him. Tossed between the rapids and the rocks like a toy, he failed desperately with the hanging tree branch. The Indian bore witness at last to the dead man's plummeting over the waterfall.

Curious, the Indian got up off his haunches and lifted his bow. Replacing it over his shoulder, he started to move again. After all, who was to say the dead man could not cheat death again? For hours now he had been at the mercy of Mother Nature. She had been toying with him. She had tossed him from one hand to another, from animal to element, and yet, the dead man had endured.

He would make a worthy opponent.

6

A REAL TERRIBLE IDEA

A whistle blares. Momma's whistle. Good timing too—my stomach is rumblin' something fierce. That's what Jonah would say so I say it too, now. Jonah reaches down a hand and I take it, grateful for the pull-up. "Come on," Jonah says. "I'll race you back to the house."

"No fair. You're bigger than me."

"I'll give you a head start."

But I don't move. I look at the pine tree and suddenly I ain't much hungry no more. The tree is all covered in scratches and my brother says that bears do the scratches to sharpen their claws or nails or whatever it is they call 'em. So they're even better at eatin' people. I ain't never seen a bear and don't plan to.

Jonah tells me to come on and pulls me by the arm. He drags me back to the house and I open the door and there's Momma.

She's all blurry but I know that she's beautiful. I can't hear what she's saying but it makes me smile anyways.

I'm sitting at the dinner table with Momma and Jonah now, a big pot in the middle of the table all steaming and smelling good. Momma nods at me to open it up and I do. I look inside and it's full of thick brown steaming stew. Lumps of meat and orange carrots floating in there, waiting for me to eat them up. My stomach growls like a grizzly.

Momma spoons us all out a bowlful each and does an extra one for the empty seat at the table. I reach for a spoon but freeze as a huge hand rests on my shoulder.

"That ain't your spoon, son," comes the curt and gruff voice of Poppa. I don't dare move. Poppa sits down at the empty seat at the table and tosses a hunk of wood and his carving knife in front of me. "It's about time you made your own."

I say nothing. I only dare to stare at him. He doesn't have a face either, but not like Momma's. Hers is blurry on not being able to remember. But I know she's beautiful. Poppa's ain't like that; his is all scratched away.

Because I want to forget.

"What's the matter, boy?" Poppa asks. "Don't go telling me you forgot how to whittle now."

"Jeremiah," Momma's sweet voice intervenes, "why don't you—"

Poppa's eyes dagger her. "You will speak when I tell you to, woman." Poppa's words are just as sharp, too. Momma shrinks back, suddenly really interested in her dinner.

I want to say something. I want to tell him I hate him. But the words just won't come.

"Answer me, boy." Poppa's tone turns mean.

I swallow. Hard.

"Jesse. Jesse? JESSE—"

~

"J*esse!*"

Jesse's eyes fluttered open. He coughed and sputtered water from his mouth and rolled onto his back. Gasping for air, he looked around. He was on the riverbank., among the stones. His legs were submerged in the water. He saw no sign of the waterfall.

How far have I been carried?

"Oh, pretty far, Jess," Jonah said. The ghostly presence of Jesse's older brother stood over him. "Nice of you to finally wake up. I been callin' your name plenty."

"Appreciate the wake-up call," Jesse said with a wince. He pushed himself onto his knees, and then to his feet. He was completely soaked through, and yet, he felt no cold. He supposed he should have been shivering. The sun was on the wane; temperatures were surely on their way down too. His teeth should have been chattering away.

Oh, hell.

He gingerly touched the cut on his forehead and pulled his finger away immediately with a wince. It felt mighty warm and incredibly painful to touch. He was getting a fever. If Jesse didn't find help before the infection took a hold of him, he would be a dead man. When before he'd had the day and night, now he'd be lucky if he had hours. If that fever started up hard, it would burn through him faster than wildfire.

Jesse's stomach warbled. What he wouldn't give for some biscuits and gravy right about now. Hell, he'd settle for some prairie oysters at this point. He couldn't afford to be getting all fussy about his food now.

Jesse checked his holster and patted himself down.

"Yep, your gun's gone, little brother," Jonah said. He was inspecting stones, picking up the occasional one and tossing them into the river. "Not bad though, for saying that's all you lost."

"Helpful as always, Jonah," Jesse said. "I look ill to you?"

Jonah paused his stone-throwing. He eyed his brother, craning his head forward as he did. "You're lookin' a little red. And that cut don't look too pretty, either," Jonah said. He dropped the rock he was holding and thrust his hands into his pockets. "You feelin' any hot?"

"Nope. Not one bit."

"Huh," Jonah said. "Might just end up buying you a little time. Cold keeping your fever down and all."

"Or I just can't feel it and I'm gonna die of either infection or pneumonia."

"Well, with that attitude, of course y'are, Jess!" Jonah

took on a lecturing tone. "Come on now. What's your plan?"

Jesse pulled the knife Frank had given him from his boot. "I lost my weapon. I need to make myself a new one."

∽

JESSE DRAGGED the knife down the tip again. With each pull, slivers of wood curled off the sharpened point of the spear. Minutes before, it had been a branch. He'd found it strewn on the bed and picked it up. Satisfied with its thickness and heft, Jesse had taken to work on the branch. Roughly six feet in length, he'd planed off one end into a sharp and deadly tip.

Keeping himself to the trees again, he was now traveling once more, keeping close to the river as a guide. Jesse had been walking about an hour, feeling no ill effects of the cold or his fever; the two seemed to be fighting each other into a stalemate. It wouldn't stay like that forever, though. He needed to get back to Bleaker's. The quicker the better.

He passed a tree and stopped. Looking down, he spied a rope haphazardly covered in leaves and mud. He chose his steps carefully and rounded the rope, before uncovering the looping snare. Jesse had an eye for the traps now. He pulled his knife and put it to the rope, disarming the trap. These snares wouldn't stop anything in this forest that would be a threat to the mountain men. All they'd do is cause the needless suffering and slow death of an innocent animal. Jesse would not be a party to that.

What the hell is that sound?

It was faint but definitely there. A soft whimper carried on the breeze. Somewhere through the trees ahead something or someone was hurting. Jesse readied his spear and ventured toward it. Through the shrubs and foliage, he encountered no other traps, but when he came upon the source of the pained whimpering, Jesse had cause to hesitate.

Caught in the rusted iron tusks of a bear trap, teeth bared in a desperate growl, hackles up, and fur on end: a wolf. Its body was spread low in as best a pouncing position as it could muster. The fur on the wolf's hind leg was knotted with dark and dried blood, the bear trap's mouth firmly clamped around its thigh. The animal was shaking. Maybe due to fear, maybe hunger, or blood loss.

Hell, I can't go leaving him like this.

Jesse moved a step closer, and the growl got louder. Saliva dripped from its upturned lips and the wolf's bloodshot eyes widened.

"It's okay," Jesse said in a soft, hushed voice. "It's okay. I'm not gonna hurt you." He gently lowered his spear to the ground. He stayed low on his haunches, as much as it pained him to do. He needed the wolf to calm down. He needed to show it he wasn't a threat. He lowered his head, almost bowed, and avoided making eye contact.

Slowly, Jesse took a step forward. He waited for the elevated growling to settle down again, soothing the animal with shushes and whispered reassurances that it would all be okay. He took another step and repeated the process. And then another. And another.

Jesse was within a foot of the wolf now. He reached out an arm to put on its back. The wolf snapped at him, and Jesse eased back slightly. He didn't pull his arm back. He knew the wolf couldn't reach him from that angle; its movement had been limited by the trap. It snapped again and again, growling more ferociously than ever. Jesse waited, shushing and repeating his assurances smoothly.

The wolf stopped snapping, but it continued to growl at him. Jesse placed his hand softly on the wolf's back and started to stroke it gently. The wolf stopped growling. To Jesse, it seemed as if the creature was in a state of shock. It didn't know what to do.

"See, buddy. I told you I was a friend, now. Feels nice, don't it?" Jesse said. He put his other hand on the wolf. With each stroke, he kept up his soothing words and slowly worked his hands back toward the trap. As he got closer to the bloodied leg, Jesse could see the wolf's top lip start to curl again.

The dog snapped as Jesse put a hand on the jaw of the trap. "Easy, easy there, friend. I told you, I'm here to help. You go biting me, I ain't gonna be able to free you now, will I? And that won't go suiting either of us." Jesse placed his other hand on the other jaw. "Okay now, what I'm gonna do is pull on this trap enough so you can get free, okay? It's gonna hurt real bad. So I'm gonna ask that you don't turn and bite me, okay? I'm *helping* you."

"This is a real terrible idea, Jesse," Jonah said.

"Shut up, Jonah." Jesse kept his eyes on the wolf and then started to count, "Okay. One... two... *three!*" Jesse pulled his arms away with all his strength. The rusted steel whined, and the wolf howled as the teeth pulled away from its leg. The wolf shot free of the trap. Jesse let go immediately and threw himself backward.

On the ground, he looked up at the wolf. No more than a lunge away, his spear out of reach, there was no way he could get to his knife in time to defend himself. Jesse stared into the wolf's almond-shaped eyes. Unmoving and icy-yellow, they regarded him back as it considered its rescuer's fate.

The wolf turned and limped away.

Jesse let out a breath he wasn't aware he was holding. He lay back on the ground for a moment and waited for his racing heart to slow back down a little.

"I told you it was the right thing to do," Jonah said.

This time Jesse shot his brother a frown. "Oh, you sure did, Big Brother. Ever with the positive outlook." Jesse stood up and brushed himself off. His clothes were almost dry now, but still, the dirt stuck to him. Jesse retrieved his spear and got to walking again.

"You reckon it'll be okay?" Jonah asked, walking next to him.

"I don't know. I never really got a good look at his leg. If it's broken, I doubt it."

"He was limping pretty bad," Jonah said, glumly.

"Doesn't necessarily mean a break. You try walking fine with a bleeding leg." Jesse was trying to be reassuring, then remembered he was talking to himself. "Anyway, he's a lot better now than he was five minutes ago. Can't do much more'n that now."

An all-too-familiar roar rang out from behind him. The hair on the back of Jesse's neck stood up. He looked back and saw nothing. Yet. He looked to his brother, who had disappeared again. Jesse looked around for an escape route, but he saw nothing but trees. The river wouldn't be an option this time; around here the current wasn't particularly strong, and if Black Fang could swim, it would easily catch Jesse in these calm waters. He did not want to find out.

Then Jesse looked *up*. Hearing another roar that sent a shiver down his spine, he knew he didn't have time to waste. Leaving his spear on the ground—there was no way he could climb with it in hand—Jesse started to clamber up the tree. Using branches for purchase, it was just like being a kid again. He managed to ascend at least ten feet off the ground before settling himself onto a branch. Looking down, he waited.

He heard the thumping steps first. Then up ahead he saw the big brown shape brush through shrubbery and trees. Black Fang bounded into the area and descended upon the bloody bear trap instantly.

Bears do have good noses, after all.

Jesse looked on, keeping his breath still as the bear's snout twitched at the trap. Jesse chided himself and wished he had reset the damned thing. The way Black Fang was sniffing at the bloodied iron, the big bear looked stupid enough to trigger it again. Black Fang snorted a dissatisfied grunt as if it had expected more. Had it been the scent of blood that had attracted it, or had it been the wolf's whines and growls? Jesse wondered. The bear swung its head from side to side.

It looked right up at Jesse.

Oh, hell.

Black Fang let out a formidable roar and charged at the tree. Jesse held on to the trunk, bracing himself as the bear crashed into the tree below. He felt the shock of the reverberations as leaves showered all around him. The bear reared up and struck the tree once more. The force shook Jesse from his perch and he cried out as he fell from the tree. Jesse rolled into the impact as he hit the ground. He scrambled forward, grabbed his spear, and then spun to face Black Fang.

There would be no running this time.

Black Fang dropped to all fours and rounded the tree.

Slimy globs of saliva trickled from its mouth as it pawed its way toward Jesse. He held the spear up and backed away steadily, not taking his eyes off the bear.

Frantically, his mind worked to try and figure out some way out of this mess. Jesse kept his spear up and his feet moving backward as his mind kept coming up empty.

Black Fang lunged its seven hundred pounds of mass and Jesse dove to his left. The bear smashed into the ground where Jesse had been and swiped around with its claws, inches away from Jesse's back.

Jesse took off at a sprint and could feel the vibrations in the ground of Black Fang beginning its pursuit. Jesse jumped for the cover of a tree just as Black Fang launched itself to strike. He felt the crunch of the impact through the tree. Jesse stepped back and saw the trunk was splintered at the base, and now stood at a new angle.

Something huge and furry swiped at Jesse's side. It felt like being kicked by a horse as he was sent rolling across the dirt. Fire bloomed in Jesse's chest as he righted himself. He did his best to bite away the pain, just as Black Fang reached him. The huge bear's frame cast such a shadow that Jesse thought it was nightfall. The bear opened its mouth and brought it down on Jesse.

He plunged the spear into its chest. Black Fang roared with fury and pain. Jesse rammed the spear farther. He felt the resistance of muscle and bone as he jerked the spear again and again. Black Fang's agonized growl grew louder.

It drew back on its hind legs, lifting Jesse off the floor. It swung a powerful paw at him. Jesse let go of the spear just before it hit him. The ground knocked the air from his lungs and the bear snapped the spear with its powerful claw.

Winded, Jesse tried his best to get to his feet, but his strength had left him. Black Fang dropped back down again and roared triumphantly. Did Black Fang know it had him beaten? Unhurried, the bear took slow, pounding steps toward Jesse. He desperately willed his unresponsive limbs to move as he tried to pull in painful gasps of air into his spasming lungs.

An arrow lodged itself into Black Fang's neck. Seconds later, another one sank into its shoulder. Black Fang erupted into another painful roar as two more hit its flank. The bear turned and bounded away from Jesse, tearing through the forest away from the raining arrows.

Jesse lay there gasping, stunned. He wasn't quite sure if what he was seeing was real. He had been seconds away from death. And now the bear was gone. Driven away by arrows from where exactly?

Jesse looked to where the arrows had come from. His newfound optimism soon faded when he saw where they had come from. In the tree line, walking toward Jesse with his bow in hand was the stranger who had watched him on his way into Bleaker's Creek with Dixie Rhodes.

Oh, hell.

Sweating, his heart racing, and his pulse pounding, Jesse found new energy as he pulled the knife from his boot and stood up to face this new threat. Once the stranger stepped into range, Jesse darted forward and lashed the blade toward him. The Indian side-stepped the attack. He then jabbed a left fist into Jesse's midriff, once again knocking the air from his lungs. As Jesse wheezed, his attacker followed the blow with a right hook that caught Jesse squarely on the jaw.

Jesse's world went dark before he'd even hit the ground.

7

PARDON ME, VENOMOUS?

Jesse opened his eyes and saw stars salting the obsidian sky. His head burned and his jaw ached as he lay on the dirt. He felt warmth to his right. He sat up and saw the dancing flames of a campfire. Somebody was tending to it, his back to Jesse.

Up close, the Indian was even bigger. He was easily a foot taller than Jesse. A long breechcloth covered his leggings above the knees, and his scuffed moccasins were caked in mud. A long, thick braid dropped between his powerful shoulders, while the sides of his head were shaved bare. He turned to Jesse and he could see the white crescent moon of a scar above his left ear, the defined cheekbones, and the thin line of a mouth. Maybe the man was cut from stone, after all.

The Indian pointed at Jesse with his long knife. "Don't

move," he said. His words were short and sharp. In his other hand, he held a small wooden cup. The Indian rose to his full six feet plus and walked over to Jesse. Kneeling to him, he offered the cup. "Drink."

Jesse took it and hovered his nose over the cup, wincing at the acrid smell. "W-what is it?" Jesse asked in a croaky voice he couldn't quite believe was his own.

"It will help."

Jesse again caught a whiff of the unsavory liquid. "And what if I don't?"

"You will die." The Indian pointed to Jesse's head. "Because of that." Jesse went to touch the wound, but the Indian put up a hand in a stopping gesture. "Do not touch. I have cleaned it. You will undo that. Drink. And rest. Then we will eat."

Jesse took a sip of the hot liquid. It had all the bite of liquor, the tang of lemon, and something ungodly in flavor. He didn't even want to think what it was. *No way to do this but to get it done though*, he thought. Jesse pinched his nose, emptied the contents of the cup into his mouth, and swallowed. He breathed through the burning down his throat and then held that breath through the incredibly strong urge to vomit. He kept swallowing until he couldn't feel it climbing its way back up his esophagus.

Once his stomach had settled, Jesse looked around. They were high up, he knew that. He could see the mountains across from him, and below, the river looked little more than a stream. On the fire, what looked like a rabbit slowly cooked on a skewer. The fact that it was now nighttime meant he'd been knocked out (again) for quite a few hours. Judging by his new friend's hospitality, he would not be moving again until morning. Jesse just hoped that whatever he had drunk would keep him alive until then.

"What was in that cup, you mind me asking?" Jesse asked.

The Indian added another log to the fire.

"Look, I still got my scalp, so I know that if you were in the business of killing me, I'd already be dead. So why don't we just dispense with the pleasantries and get right on down to why we're doing what we're doing?"

The Indian glanced at Jesse, then returned his attention to the fire. Jesse noted the coat he was wearing. Tattered and old, one sleeve was missing at the shoulder, and the other ended at the elbow. It was on that arm that he noted the chevrons of a sergeant's insignia. Jesse had heard of Cheyenne that had served in the army. They'd done it for land and to fight other tribes, the whole 'enemy of my enemy is my friend' idea. He'd never actually seen one in the flesh, though. It could have been just as likely he'd killed the sergeant and taken it as a trophy, for all Jesse knew.

Jesse shivered, realizing he could feel the cold again. For the discomfort it brought, he was grateful. First from the bear, now from infection, that was twice this man had saved Jesse, assuming his medicine would keep working, that is. And here he was judging the man he didn't know, based on a coat he wore, instead of the actions that had kept him alive.

"Thank you," Jesse said. "Not just for the drink and my head, but the bear too. I'd be dead twice over now if not for you."

The Indian turned the skewered rabbit as he said, "You're welcome."

"I'm Jesse Clayton. Might I know the name of the man who saved me?" The Indian shot Jesse a look that had him thinking the man may just have been regretting his earlier actions, now that he was faced with conversation. "Or we can just sit here and enjoy the stars until dinner's ready."

"Nodin."

"Pardon me?" Jesse said.

"My name is Nodin. And you are welcome... Jesse," Nodin said. He stood up and lifted the rabbit from the fire. He peeled away one of the legs and Jesse watched the glistening flesh tear away with ease. Saliva flooded his mouth. Nodin handed Jesse the rest of the animal on the skewer. "No more talking. Eat now. Then sleep. In the morning, we will talk."

"I appreciate that, Nodin, but I really should—"

"If you leave now, I will not stop you. But I will not save you again. You will die."

Jesse took the skewered rabbit and nodded. "Okay. I

won't argue there." Jesse bit into the rabbit. Boy, did it taste good.

~

Jesse flinched out of his slumber and immediately narrowed his eyes at the light of the rising sun. He'd dreamt of his old home again, down South and out in the woods. His father had been in his dream again, along with his mother and Jonah. The two of them had watched helplessly as once again Jesse had been scolded by Poppa. Over what, he wasn't quite sure; the memory of it was slipping away from him, like sand through his fingers, as dreams often had their way of doing.

He sat up, feeling a soreness run through him he hadn't felt since being thrown around like a toy by Slim Joe Cullen. He winced as he stretched out his limbs, but the worst of the pain came from the throbbing in his head.

"Drink," Nodin said, next to him, handing Jesse another cup of the acrid horror water.

Jesse took it. "Much obliged," he said, before pinching his nose and tipping it back, swallowing it in three big, disgusting gulps. Jesse then waited for that awful rise in his stomach to settle. "Oh, that just gets worse every time."

"How do you feel?"

"A few aches and pains, which is pretty lucky considering this past day. I wish the drums in my head would quieten, mind."

Nodin regarded Jesse like he'd spoken another language. "I do not follow."

Jesse laughed. "Right, uh... let's just say I've got a fierce headache still, okay?"

Nodin nodded once. "Very well. Your headache is of concern. You may need something stronger than what I can give you. Where are you going?"

"Back to Bleaker's Creek, if you know it."

"We can be there by this afternoon," Nodin said. He stood up and kicked mud onto the dying fire, before stamping out the embers with his moccasins. "We leave now." Nodin offered Jesse his hand. Obliging, he felt the strength of the Indian as he was pulled up. Jesse waited a moment as a moderate swaying dizziness overcame him again, glad that it was not as bad as it had been the night before. He looked forward to a proper bed. And a meal, too.

They began to walk.

∼

IT HAD BEEN an hour or so in silence, Jesse struggling to keep up with his savior, limping across the uneven ground. The whole time he'd been trying to figure Nodin out, trying to understand the reasoning for his current situation. Eventually, Jesse just decided to go ahead and ask.

"Why'd you decide to save me? That bear could've just as easily torn you apart as he was about to me."

"Not likely."

"Oh," Jesse said, not expecting such a response. "I'm not sure I'm following you there, friend."

"That bear nears its long slumber for the winter. At this moment it is at its most ferocious and dangerous, but it is also at its most defensive. My arrows caused it enough discomfort to realize it would be better to find food elsewhere. Risking more harm for your head would complicate its safe hibernation."

"You knew where to hurt it."

Nodin nodded.

"You know these mountains well then," Jesse said.

"No. These mountains are not mine. But Mother Nature's design never wavers. A mountain is just a mountain. A bear... a bear."

"Well, don't that just sound poetic."

"You mock me," Nodin said, not looking back. His pace may have even quickened a little.

"No, not at all, Nodin... It's just that you make it all sound so easy. Driving off bears and tracking people. And saving my life. Thing is, it keeps bugging me that I can't figure out why."

"Why what?"

"Why you saved me."

Nodin stopped and turned to Jesse. "It was not my

intent. I watched you on your travels in the stagecoach, your stand-off with those mountain-dwelling murderers, and then I watched you get shot in the head and fall to your apparent death."

"You saw that?"

"I did. I then traveled to where you fell, with the intent of taking whatever was worth taking." Nodin stopped, expecting a response. "Instead, I found you alive. I was curious."

"That's... probably not worth dwelling on too much. You find my hat?"

"I did not. I decided to follow you, and I saw your encounters with the traps and the wolves, the bear and the venomous spider—"

"Pardon me, venomous? The little black thing with the red butt?"

Nodin nodded again.

"Ha! Told you!" Jonah cried from behind a tree.

"Quiet, you!" Jesse spat at his brother. He then saw the concerned regard Nodin now afforded him. Jesse cleared his throat. "Shall we?" Jesse said. He gestured ahead and they began walking again. "Anyway, you thought I was dead. I wasn't and you decided to follow?"

"I was intrigued. And then I saw you spare the wolf when there was no benefit to you whatsoever. Tell me, Jesse Clayton, why did you do so? Surely you knew the danger it posed."

"I did. But I'm also a man who believes in doing what's right if he's in such a position."

"Even at potential harm to yourself?"

Jesse had to think about that. At the time, he'd been operating on a mix of adrenaline, instinct, and a hefty dose of delirium. He thought about how he'd put it, the feeling he had felt when he had looked into that poor, defenseless wolf's eyes and just known it would all work out. "Maybe it was the bang to the head talking, maybe I was just being naïve, having never really been one for the mountain life, but I got... a sense that it wouldn't hurt me."

Nodin scoffed. "It was the bang to your head. You were lucky. I have seen many of you whites in my time, and only a handful have ever treated this place with any kind of respect. Like those men who tried to murder you, most would not help the wolf. They would probably worsen its suffering."

Jesse nodded slowly. "Sad to say that I know the kind of folks'd do that, too. But that's why you helped me? Because I saved a wolf?"

"That may be why Mother Nature grants you mercy this day, Jesse Clayton. I am only following her lead," Nodin said, he then turned back to walking again.

Jesse took a deep breath and clambered after him. This was much more of an effort for him in his weakened state. As he struggled, his thoughts turned to the mountain men.

A question occurred to Jesse. "The two men that shot me. Have you seen them do this kind of thing before?"

"For some months now, they have preyed on those who would travel through these mountains.

"The woman I was with, did you see what happened to her?"

"They took her."

Jesse stopped. "Wait! Where?" Nodin turned with a look of frustration. Clearly, he wasn't enjoying the heavy dialogue and slow progress of their walk. Jesse didn't care.

"Farther up this very mountain, they have a small shack," Nodin said. "She will be there. And alive. When they have taken women before, they have sold them to eastern tribes."

"And you've never thought to stop them?"

"I have my reasons for being here. The trouble of the white man is not my worry," Nodin said as he attempted to turn away again.

Jesse rounded Nodin and blocked his path. "But you helped me! If she's still alive, we have to help her."

Nodin seemed much taller as he towered over Jesse. Shadows fell across his features, giving the Indian an even more intimidating appearance. "It is not my concern. Get out of my way."

"*No.*" Jesse made his best attempt at echoing his imposing disposition. "We have to help."

"Why?"

"The same reason I helped the damned wolf, Nodin."

Nodin's lip flattened and the cords in his shoulders tightened. Then he relaxed. "Fine. I will help you, Jesse Clayton. But know this: if we are delayed too long, your fever will return. It will burn through your body much faster and consume you entirely. And there will be nothing you nor I can do. You will die."

Jesse didn't even hesitate. "That's a risk I'm willing to take, Nodin. Now let's go."

∽

THE SHACK WAS A VERY loose term for what Jesse saw. Built with a series of very haphazardly assembled logs and greened by patches of moss, the corners crumbled with rot. It bore no windows, only a roughly cut door frame. The roof was crooked and so was its chimney. Smoke chugged from the top of it, wisping up into the air.

"Looks like somebody's home, at least," Jesse said.

"Agreed," Nodin replied.

Crouched and peering out from a huge oak, Jesse could see the stagecoach was there. Its wheels had been removed and the wagon itself was in a state of partial deconstruction. The mountain men liked to get use out of everything, it appeared. The horses were tethered next to it, lapping at the mossy log walls.

"Be wary of the traps," Nodin said, pointing out several

bear traps and snares. Jesse had been oblivious to all of them, being so focused on the dwelling of his attempted murderers.

"Thanks, Nodin, I had no idea. So how are we gonna play this?"

"This is not a game, Jesse Clayton."

Jesse shook his head, biting back the need to explain himself. "What do we *do*?"

"We take either side of the shack. I'll stir up the horses to draw one of them out. Take him down without a sound. Wait for the other to come out. Deal with him."

"Simple. I like it."

The two of them moved silently through the trees and around the traps, then split off from each other as they rounded the shack. They met up again moments later on either side of the front. Jesse readied his knife and gave Nodin a nod. The Indian picked up a stone and tossed it at one of the horses. It struck the horse on the nose and the animal whinnied and reared, pulling against the tethering post.

Inside, Jesse heard voices. Although he could not discern exactly what discourse was partaking, they sounded annoyed. Nodin waved Jesse back and the two of them retreated around the corners.

Jesse peered out as the bigger of the two mountain men emerged from the shack. Otis, in his buckskin suit—and Jesse's Stetson, its rim bent horribly out of shape—trudged out. He yelled at the horse to shut up, and just as he got to the corner, Nodin burst out and thrust his forearm into the big man's chin. Otis staggered back and Nodin pounced on him, pushing the mountain man to the ground. Jesse watched as Nodin suddenly froze. His eyes were fixed on a leather necklace that fell around Otis' neck.

"Where... where did you—"

Otis slammed a fist into Nodin's head and the Indian fell away.

Jesse rushed toward the pair of them. As he crossed the doorway he felt something cold press into his neck.

"Move even an inch, sonny, and I'll be pickin' bits of your brain outta these here trees," Wilbur said. After which, Jesse heard the familiar clicking of a hammer pulling back.

8

NOW OR NEVER

No sooner than he'd pulled the gun away, Wilbur had thrust Jesse into the shack. Inside was a fireplace, on either side of which were cots. On one of those was a very scared, very bound Joan. Her pleasant demeanor of before had been torn to pieces along with her dress, as she curled up wide-eyed in her undergarments. Her eyes were puffy and pleading. Jesse thought she recognized him, but that was hard to tell, given his rather disheveled state and the dank rag stuffed into her mouth.

"It's okay, Joan. It's me, Jesse. I'm here to help," Jesse said.

"No, you ain't, sonny," Wilbur said, almost gleefully. "All you've gone and done is gotten yourself and your native friend dead. Sit." Wilbur gestured with the pistol and Jesse sat down on the cot opposite Joan. Jesse leaned forward and casually slipped a hand across the top of his boot, smiling at Joan as he did. "We are mighty grateful to you though, friend. Bringing that annoying savage to us, and saving us a whole lotta trouble," Wilbur added.

Jesse felt a wave of heat roll throughout his body as the fever began its creeping return. He had to hold back a laugh at its wonderful sense of timing. He smiled at Wilbur through it; now was the time to exude calm, not weakness.

"Hey, Otis," Wilbur called over his shoulder, not taking his eyes or his Smith & Wesson off Jesse. "How are ya doing with that Injun?"

"He ain't goin' nowhere. He's all tied up."

"Good. Come 'ere."

Otis lumbered over to the shack until his big frame darkened the doorway. "We killin' him?" "Not us. Take him to Bleaker's," Wilbur said and then reached down beneath Joan's cot, keeping his gun trained on Jesse. He pulled out the shredded remains of Joan's dress and handed it to Otis. "Take this and the native down to the Creek. Let them put it together about her and the dirt-worshipper, then be sure to help them lynch the damned fool from the nearest tree."

"But what if he talks?"

"Either gag him or bust him so he *can't*. Or better yet, get them all riled to do the beatin' for ya. Tell 'em you caught him tryin' take her back to his tribe."

"You got it. What about them two?"

Wilbur grinned. "Her, we can finally have our fun with,

tonight. Then we can take her tomorrow to them natives out east we sold the others to. But him? What do you think: snare or bear trap?"

Otis chuckled. "Bear trap every time, Wil. That sucker can scream and wish that bullet had hit him lower. Still can't believe the son of a bitch is alive."

"I know," Wilbur said. "It really is our lucky day, isn't it?" Wilbur flashed a smile of filthy teeth. "Now go on and git. I don't wanna be waiting too long, or I'll start on her without you." Wilbur watched Joan recoil as he said this and licked his lips. Jesse fought back the urge to dive at him there and then.

No, Clayton. You play it cool, now. Wait for Otis to ride away and even the odds a little.

Light flooded back into the shack again as Otis left. Jesse heard him grunt as he shifted Nodin, then a moment later the clattering of horse hooves steadily fade into the distance.

"You rest easy there, darlin'. I'll be with you real soon," Wilbur said. The twiggy old bastard then turned to Jesse. "You. Stand up."

Jesse did.

"Step outside."

Jesse did.

"Turn right and start walking."

Jesse did. He looked around for anything he could use to his advantage. The passing foliage and trees offered up nothing. He hadn't been able to fish his blade from his boot, and he could feel the deathly presence of the gun aimed at his head. He saw the bear trap ahead, laying open-mouthed and beckoning its metal teeth, waiting to devastate him.

Jesse needed an idea. He needed it thirty seconds ago.

Maybe his luck had finally run out. As he walked toward an untimely and undoubtedly slow death, his aching and frantic mind failed to come up with some clever sleight of hand or whimsy trick to upend the man with a gun pointed at him. Maybe it was the fever starting to cook his insides again, but Jesse figured perhaps he didn't need anything fancy to get him out of it. The answer may just be as simple as it was stupid.

A few feet from the trap, Jesse stopped.

"I tell you to stop, sonny?"

"No."

"Then what the hell're you doin'? Git to walkin'."

"Why?"

"Excuse me? 'Cause I said so, idjit!"

Jesse turned around, hands raised on either side of his head. He saw the dumbstruck awe etched into the lines on Wilbur's withered face. "The way I see it, there's two ways this goes," Jesse said, "and me, being a man who isn't much for discomfort, would rather choose a bullet to the head and a quick death, as opposed to being served up to the wolves with a busted ankle."

"You think I give a shit?"

"You think I give a shit about *you* giving a shit? You want me in that bear trap yonder, you're gonna have to drag me into it."

Wilbur snarled at Jesse. "You think I'm playin'?" he thumbed back the hammer on his Smith & Wesson. "Fine. You want to die. I can just as sure make it slow," Otis said, training his gun on different appendages: first Jesse's arm, then a leg. "Maybe I'll plug each limb and let you bleed out that way. I know where to shoot a man so as not to bleed him too quick, see."

Come on, asshole, give me an opening. One last roll of the die, that's all I need.

"You sure you can hit me at this range? I know it's a touch closer than before," Jesse said.

"Think I may just manage it this time, sonny," Wilbur said with glee, as his aim lowered toward Jesse's foot.

Now or never.

As Wilbur squeezed his finger around the trigger, Jesse took a step to his right. The gun boomed and a searing burn ran across Jesse's thigh but he was already in motion. Jesse bashed his fist down onto Wilbur's wrist and the old man cried out, losing the weapon. Jesse rammed his left elbow into Wilbur's nose and felt a satisfyingly wet crunch. Wilbur howled again and stumbled back, screaming in a rage. Jesse did not stop. He grabbed the old man's arm and throat and whirled around, upending the mountain man and throwing him.

A hefty, metallic *THUNK!* was closely followed by an almost animalistic squealing from Wilbur. The old man clutched at the jaw of the bear trap, trying to free the hand seized within its teeth. The old man's wrist turned up at an angle that was by no means natural, and his hand was already turning a dark shade of purple.

"You son of a bitch! Christ, that hurts!" Wilbur yelled in between screams. "Get me... get me outta this now, you hear me?" Wilbur growled in pain as he tugged at his trapped leg. "OTIS! Otis, you get back here, now!"

Jesse reached down for the Smith & Wesson and holstered it. "Come on now, Wilbur, surely you know how these traps work. You can—" Jesse stopped talking midsentence as his attention was suddenly held by a rustling in the foliage.

He couldn't quite believe what he saw emerging from the bushes. Brown fur, mottled with dirt and mud. Head hung low and eyes centered squarely on the two men. Lips curled back to reveal a broken and black tooth.

I guess luck swings both ways.

Jesse started to step back slowly, as Black Fang languidly pawed its way toward them. Wilbur, seeing the look on Jesse's face as he retreated, looked to what he was backing away from and his screams renewed with greater resolve.

"Help me, please! HELP GOD DAMN YOU! DON'T LET THAT DAMN BEAR GIT ME! HEEELP!" Wilbur screamed. Anger had given way to desperation.

Jesse kept retreating slowly, despite Black Fang's larger strides eating up the distance between them. If he ran, he risked provoking the bear into a chase. His only hope was that the bear remembered their earlier encounter, and that of the two men, Wilbur presented the much more convenient meal, if a little old and spoiled.

Black Fang reached Wilbur, who in his frantic mania was now tugging profusely at his trapped arm. The bear considered him and then looked up at Jesse. The bear watched as he backed away and its predatory eyes narrowed.

"Come on, you big son of a bitch, take the damned easy meal," Jesse muttered to himself.

Black Fang stepped around Wilbur, who had now stopped his screams as he noticed the bear upon him.

Jesse swallowed hard.

Black Fang turned its hefty body to Wilbur, whose screaming resumed. It swiped him with a meaty paw, pressing him to the ground. Wilbur stopped writhing, stunned by the blow. Black Fang then opened its mouth, before clamping its teeth into the mountain man's shoulder.

Jesse turned away as Wilbur screamed again.

He didn't have long.

JESSE COULDN'T RUN. He could manage a half jog, favoring his right leg, as a glance showed him that Wilbur's bullet hadn't quite been that wayward. His outer left thigh now bore a bloody gouge where the round had glanced him.

Lucky indeed.

Jesse reached the shack and wasted no time as he hobbled to Joan's cot. He pulled his knife and she recoiled from him.

"It's fine, Joan. But we don't have time. Stay still and do as I say, or we'll end up eaten by a bear," Jesse said. Whether abated or shocked, Joan stayed still as Jesse sawed through the bonds on her wrists and ankles. She pulled the cloth that had gagged her and Jesse helped her off the bed.

"You're not hurt too bad, are you?" Jesse asked.

Joan shook her head.

"All right now, come on!" Jesse said as he took her hand and jerked her out of the shack. There was no time for etiquette here.

As Jesse led her outside, he glanced over at Black Fang, who was fortunately still busying itself over Wilbur. He had ceased his screaming and lay still, only twitching and shuffling in response to the bear's biting.

Jesse led her to the horse. "Can you ride?"

"I've... I've had lessons," Joan said like her voice wasn't hers, eyes still glassy from her ordeal.

"Well, can you shoot?"

Joan shook her head.

"Get on and take the reins," Jesse said as he untied the horse. He helped Joan onto the horse and then clambered up behind her. "Let's go!"

"Where?"

"That way!" Jesse said, pointing in the direction he thought he'd heard Otis go earlier. Truthfully, he wasn't sure it was the right way and worried he may only be sending them deeper into the forest. But in that present moment, Jesse's mind was primarily concerned with putting as much distance as he could between him and Black Fang before the bear decided it fancied a second course. They could eventually find their way back to Bleaker's later, but not if they were dead.

As the horse began to canter across the grass, Jesse looked back once more over his shoulder to see Black Fang still chewing on Wilbur. The bear looked up at the fleeing horse and its quarry and Jesse held his breath. Black Fang growled, snorted, and then took another bite out of Wilbur.

9

DON'T YOU DO IT, CLAYTON

Jesse tore off a piece of his sleeve, threaded it beneath his bleeding thigh, and then tied it around his wound. He groaned as he pulled the knot tight; his vision grew blurry momentarily.

"Are you okay, Mr. Clayton?" Joan called over the pounding of the horse's hooves.

"Yep. Fine," Jesse said through gritted teeth. On top of the pain, he was aware of his profuse sweating and the intense heat he now felt in his cheeks and his chest. His exertions were fueling the spread of the infection as Nodin had predicted, but he still had time. He had full dominion over all of his faculties still, and his headache had yet to reach the agonizing levels of before.

"I'm not sure which way to ride," Joan said.

"Just keep going down the incline. We'll be sure to hit a

road soon enough, I know it." Jesse didn't know it, he only hoped. Faith and luck had served him so well these past twenty-four hours, he was beginning to take the two of them for granted. If he did indeed get out of this mess alive, he was going to hit up the craps and poker tables in Missoula. He'd get to Winona a rich man.

It wasn't long before Jesse's faith proved to be well-placed. They were riding mere minutes when the trees gave way to a dry strip of mud, well-beaten and tracked with horseshoes and wagon trails.

"All right, can you make her go faster, Joan?" Jesse said.

"Sure can," Joan replied. She flicked the reins with her wrist and yelled "YA!" The horse's canter turned into a gallop as its hooves beat its way down the dirt track. Jesse looked down the road, and in the distance, he could see the faint, rising trails of smoke that would surely be from the fires of Bleaker's Creek.

No more than a couple of miles away, Jesse only hoped they hadn't tarried too long on the mountain and still had time to save Nodin. It wouldn't take much to stoke up the fires of paranoia, and pin the mountain men's murderous endeavors on Nodin. The people of that camp had been scared for a long time. The butcher, Red, struck Jesse as the kind of man that wouldn't need much convincing to lynch Nodin from the nearest tree. Given that only days ago he'd nearly put a brace of arrows in Red's son, Kip. Not even Dieter's rational mind would be able to talk him down from it, Jesse was sure. He needed to get Joan there for all to see if he was going to quash the trouble.

"Mr. Clayton, I think there's somebody on the road up ahead," Joan said.

Jesse looked over her shoulder to see a lone rider farther up the road, between them and the town, coming toward them at a canter. As they drew closer, Jesse saw a familiar buckskin suit and a tattered Stetson hat.

A Stetson with a hole in it.

"Joan, stop the horse."

Joan pulled on the reins and the horse skidded to a halt in the dirt. Jesse hopped off.

"Listen to me now," Jesse said. "I need you to get off this road and take a nice, wide loop around, okay? Put as many trees between you and that rider as you can, you hear?"

"Why? What about you?" Joan said. "I don't much like the thought of riding alone."

"Trust me, you'll be much safer riding on your own. Like I said, a nice long loop around and then make your way to Bleaker's. It ain't much farther from here and you'll be safe. I promise."

"O—okay." Joan nodded and smiled meekly. "Goodbye, Mr. Clayton. And thank you."

"You're welcome. Goodbye, Joan."

The woman pulled the reins and the horse took off into the trees, disappearing out of sight. A moment later, the rider cantered to a stop no more than thirty paces from

Jesse, who stood with a hand resting on the butt of the Smith & Wesson he'd taken from the now well-dead Wilbur.

"Where's my uncle?" Otis said. His face was serious. His tone was deadly.

"You mean, Wilbur? He was your uncle?" Jesse said. "Ugly runs through the whole family then, does it?"

"You tell me RIGHT NOW!" Otis barked and jabbed a finger at Jesse.

"Pretty sure he's dead, Otis. Tried to put me in one o' your bear traps and wound up getting eaten by a grizzly. I think they call that *irony*. Black Fang, the big feller was called. You're aware of him, right?"

Otis's nostrils flared. The mountain man dropped from his horse and stepped toward Jesse, resting his hand on his gun now, too.

"I'll go ahead and assume yes," Jesse said. "What'd you do with Nodin?"

"Don't you worry about him. That filthy mud-worshipper is about to get what's comin' to him."

Jesse stiffened as he felt a wave of heat and dizziness run through his body. His vision rippled and he took a deep breath against the sudden rising in his stomach. Sweat dripped from his nose as he wiped away more from his chin with his sleeve.

Come on now, a few more minutes is all I need.

"Joan'll get there and straighten it all out," Jesse said, trying his best not to sound like he wanted to throw up.

"She won't be talkin' any of 'em down," Otis chuckled. "He's probably dead already. Like you're about to be. You done my uncle. Can't let that stand."

"You ain't got your uncle to distract me this time. This is just you and me, and the matter of who's faster. At this range, I've never been the slower. You done this much?"

Otis steadied himself. Jesse watched his shoulders slacken, loosening for the strike. "Once or twice..." the mountain man said as he flexed his fingers around his gun. Any second now he was going to reach for it. "...You?"

A breeze ran between the two of them.

"A few more times than twice," Jesse said.

Jesse watched as Otis's shoulder twitched.

A single shot rang out; its report echoed off the mountain.

Otis's gun clattered into the dirt. He clasped his hands to his chest like he was in some last desperate plea for repentance. Blood ran between his fingers as he fell into a sitting position. He gasped and gargled, eyes wide as he watched Jesse walk over to him.

He plucked the Stetson from the dying man's head. Jesse pulled at the brim, trying to straighten it back out, and then inspected the ragged bullet hole. He placed it back on his own head, then tipped the brim of it to Otis.

"Say hi to your uncle for me," Jesse said and walked off.

He clambered onto Otis's horse, turned it around, and then galloped down the road to Bleaker's Creek.

Otis sputtered, gasped, and burbled, then slumped sideways onto the ground. He coughed once, then wheezed his last breath.

∽

THE DIRT ROAD turned muddy as Jesse rounded into Bleaker's Creek. He realized just how much strength had slipped away from him as he struggled to keep himself atop the horse skidding in sludge.

He could hear shouting in the square. As he rode into it, he saw the crowd of almost two dozen. So taken by the event that none turned to notice Jesse's arrival. He saw Nodin, bloodied and bruised, with a noose around his neck. He was being held up by Red as his son Kip threw the other end of the rope over a tree.

Red was mid-speech as he held Nodin, "... This *heathen* will get what's coming to him! For all the terror he's caused and the people him and his kind have murdered!"

"No, Red. You must stop zis at once!" Dieter pleaded. "Zis is not how we should do things here. Never."

The crowd had sided with Red as many of them called for the doctor to shut up and be still, and to let Red do 'God's work.' Reason had abandoned these people, Jesse was ashamed to see. Kip was pulling down on the rope and

Nodin's head was starting to rise. The time for diplomacy had passed.

Jesse pulled out the Smith & Wesson, raised it above his head, and fired.

The entire camp silenced, and the crowd finally turned their attention to him.

"Jesse? You are alive?" Dieter bleated.

"What in the hell is goin' on here?" Red said, his bushy eyebrows merging into a thick, furry worm atop his brow. "Otis said you was *dead*."

"Well, I ain't, and if your boy does anything other than let go of that God-damned rope, I'm gonna put a bullet in his leg," Jesse said as he took an unfavorably shaky aim at the boy. Jesse could suddenly see three Kips, each one of them blurry as hell and dancing in his vision.

"Kip! You keep hold of that rope, boy! That bastard is with the native."

"Put that rope down, now!" Jesse yelled. The fury was back in his head and it had robbed him of his patience. Jesse cocked the pistol. "I ain't having an innocent man slain today!"

"Slain like the two o' you did that prospector and his wife you rode with?" Red said.

"What? No. Joan's alive," Jesse said, looking around for her. "She should be here. I sent her ahead." Jesse tried to blink away the blurring from his vision. With his free hand, he sleeved away the sweat that stung his eyes. "Where is she?" A feeling of dread settled in the pit of his belly. Had something happened to her? Black Fang, or the wolves?

"Can somebody shoot this asshole?" Red yelled.

"Red, calm down," Dieter chimed in again. He approached the butcher slowly, with his hands raised. "Zer is more here than we understand. Let the man free, and we can resolve this. And if true, we can make sure proper justice is done."

"Get back, Doc, this ain't time for you soft types. This slimy native'll find a way to slip free and scalp us all if we give him even half a chance. Otis said!" Red said. Several from the crowd shouted in agreement with the butcher.

"Otis also said he killed Jesse, and yet, he is still here," Dieter said.

"One last chance, Kip," Jesse called again. "I'm gonna count to three. One..." Jesse began counting as the crowd watched on. Kip looked over to his father, whose gaze only grew more fierce.

"Keep hold of that rope, boy!" Red shouted.

"Two!" Jesse's vision was becoming increasingly blurry. Of the three Kips to choose from, he decided to settle on the one in the middle. The Smith & Wesson now felt so incredibly heavy in his hand, he had to bring up his left to brace the gun and steady his aim.

"Don't you do it, Clayton. Don't you shoot my boy!"

"*Three—*"

"Wait! Waaait!" came a voice from behind Jesse. A few

seconds later, a horse passed by him and a figure was atop it. Jesse's sight was too impaired to see who it was.

"Joan!" somebody cried out, Jesse wasn't quite sure who. His vision was beginning to darken.

"Just what in the God-damned depths of the devil's abyss, is goin' on here?" Red yelled.

"Let that man go!" Joan demanded as Jesse felt the gun slip from his fingers and clatter to the ground. His eyes felt heavy and drums pounded louder than ever before in his head. "That man you have has not harmed me!"

Nodin was safe. And so was Joan. His job was done.

"It was because of him and Jesse that I live!" Joan yelled.

His eyes closed and he no longer had the strength to open them. He felt himself slipping backward and reached for the reins. He missed them and fell from the horse. The ground knocked the wind out of him, and he lay there, unable to move or breathe.

For Jesse Clayton, everything went dark.

INTERLUDE THREE

"Get him on to ze bed," said the man Jesse had called Dieter.

Nodin did as he was asked, carrying the now limp form of Jesse into the doctor's cabin. There were instruments and tools Nodin had never seen before, and he wondered just how these metal trinkets could provide greater healing than Mother Nature could. But he knew the limits of his restorative knowledge and trusted Jesse's fate to the hands of the white man and his steel remedies.

Carefully, he placed Jesse down on the canvas cot, cautious not to jar his head, which was bleeding through the dressing he had given him the night before. His left leg was also oozing blood. Nodin wondered just how much more the man could stand to lose, given how much of an ordeal he had endured already.

"Please, allow me some room," the doctor said and Nodin took a step back. The huge man that had handled him, Red, was standing inside the doorway with his cleaver, giving Nodin a look that made him want to bash the fat man's head into the wall. He had to remind himself: these people were fearful of him and mistaken. He should forgive, he thought as he held a hand to his tender and bruising neck, but that would not come easy or with haste.

The doctor put his ear to Jesse's chest and held it there. After a moment he pulled away and said, "He is still breathing. Zat is good." The doctor then addressed Red. "If you could show our friend here... I do apologize, mein freund," Dieter said to Nodin, "but in all the drama and disarray I was never able to attain your name. If you would?"

"Nodin."

"Ah, ya! Nodin, it is a pleasure, mein name is Dieter Kraus. I believe you have met Red here already. Who I'm sure will treat you much more... kindly going forward." Dieter then addressed Red. "If you could show Nodin here to ze hotel and my wife, please Red?" Then to Nodin again, "I'm sure you need something to eat and a place to sleep. Allow my wife to look after you. You are very welcome to stay. As a token of apology at the very least!"

"I'd rather stay with my..." Nodin paused. "Jesse."

"I am sure that you would, and I commend you for that, ya," the doctor said. "Alas, I need time and space to be able to properly treat him. Please, go and sleep. Later, when you are rested and Jesse is stable, I will come and find you and apprise you of everything."

"Very well," Nodin said. He took one last look at Jesse, and then followed Red out of the doctor's quarters.

~

Nodin sat in front of the fire in the square, elbows resting on his knees and hands clasped in front of his face, and watched the sky. He'd been there long enough to see the sun retreat behind the mountains and see the moon emerge from its slumber in the darkness.

Dieter approached him and asked if he could share the log he sat upon. Nodin dipped his head once. The doctor thanked him and sat down.

"My wife says you will not sleep in your room. Is there a problem with ze bed?"

"I am more comfortable out here."

The doctor nodded a little too zealously. "Of course, of course. You ate well at least, she said. Had a second helping of her stew."

"It was good."

"That I most certainly agree with you on."

"How is he?" Nodin asked.

Dieter offered Nodin a pained smile while he thought about what to say. "Straight to the point, aren't you?" the doctor said, followed by a nervous chuckle. He took in a deep breath and then sighed. "It is not good. Was it you that treated him, initially?"

"I did."

"And a good job you did. Without zat aid, Jesse would most certainly not have lived through yesterday, let alone come as far as he did today. He has you to thank for zat. But in his... labors, ze wounds he has sustained, ze blood loss and fever, I'm afraid he is in a rather bad shape. The infection has taken a good hold of him, and he has lost a lot of blood. As a result, he is in what we call a coma. Do you know what zat is?"

"I do not," Nodin said, eyes still on the sky.

"His body is in a kind of sleep. A prolonged state of unconsciousness zat ze body will succumb to when subjected to severe injury and illness. I am doing what I can and when I can, but... I'm afraid zat what happens next, whether he will pull through or pass on, all rests on him now."

"He will pull through."

"Ha! Mein freund, you seem so sure of him! I'll bet he is quite ze resilient fellow, but I do wonder if he may have undergone too much for his body to come back from."

"He will pull through."

"If I may ask, mein freund, what makes you so sure?"

Nodin turned to the doctor. "I have seen him cheat death once. I have seen him encounter the great grizzly that resides in these mountains and live. He survived with little more than a blade and his own cunning. A fever will not be the end of him."

"Great grizzly? Do you mean Black Fang?"

"Is that what you call it? The bear with the missing tooth?"

"Ya."

"That very beast."

"*Mein Gott*," Dieter said.

10

I'D RATHER NOT DIE TODAY

"Jesse, you go on and get your coat on now," Momma says. Her voice is just the most wonderful thing. So soothing and sweet. I stand there, watching her throwing clothes into a trunk and slamming it shut, then moving over to her dresser and pulling it out. Reaching behind, she shouts for Jonah to get my coat. She isn't mean about it. Not like Poppa. Her tone is gentle and understanding. And I love her for that. She pulls out a bag that jingles as she hefts its weight in her hand, and then she tosses that onto the trunk.

Suddenly, I am blanketed in darkness.

"Come on, stupid. Get your coat on!" Jonah says. "We don't got long until Poppa gets back."

I pull the coat off my head and wrangle with it until I can get my arms into my sleeves, a difficult task for a seven-year-old. Momma comes over and kneels to me. Her dark hair is pulled back into a bun atop her head, but her face is still a mystery to me. She untucks my collar and pats it down, before settling a peck on my forehead. "Come on, Jesse. It's time to go."

"Go where?" I ask.

"Somewhere new. Where we can start afresh," Momma says as she takes my hand and leads me out of the doorway.

"Someplace without Poppa," Jonah adds. Momma scowls at him and he goes real quiet real quick.

Outside there's a wagon waiting, a man sitting up front with a big gun laying across his lap. He's got greasy hair and a long nose, and half of his ear missing!

"We're ready, Lonnie," Momma says. She throws the trunk in the back of the wagon. She reaches down to lift me when she's stopped by what her friend says in reply.

"We got a problem. Up the road yonder."

Momma stood back up and I saw her face turn real pale. It was like her eyes sank and her smile just melted away. It made my chest hurt. "It's him, isn't it?" Momma says flatly.

"It sure as shit ain't President Johnson," Lonnie answers.

The rider on the horse gets closer, and I squeeze Momma's hand as tight as I can when I see who it is.

"The hell are you doin' here, Compton?" Poppa says. His voice is gritty and mean.

Lonnie moves the big gun toward Poppa. "Come to take my cousin away from you, Jeremiah. There ain't gonna be a problem, I don't suppose?"

"That depends on my wife," Poppa says. Momma bends

down to pick me up. "You put him back down. Now. You can go just fine if that's what you want to go an' do. That's one o' two ways this goes. The other is you try and take my boys away. You try that and I'll gun you down, bitch."

"I'm taking my boys, Jeremiah," Momma says.

"Try it and I'll put a bullet in them, too." Did Poppa really just say he'd kill us?

"You wouldn't," Momma says.

Poppa moves his hand toward his gun. He don't really say much since he's been home from the big war he says he'd been fightin' in. But he's been quicker to do bad things. Especially to Momma. She lifts me back down and I grab onto her dress. I don't wanna let go.

"No, Momma, don't leave!" I say.

"I'm not going anywhere, sweetie. I'm—"

"Yes, y'are," Poppa says. "You want to leave? Go. You done made your choice, you either leave now with your cousin or this ends bloody, Alberta."

"Jeremiah, I'll—"

"Get gone. NOW."

"I'd rather not die today, cousin," Lonnie says. "Get in already."

Momma glances down at me and Jonah. I can feel my eyes stinging as Momma peels away my hands, kisses them both, and gently places them at my sides. I try to move back to her but Jonah wraps his arms around me. "It's okay, Jesse. It's okay. Momma'll come back," Jonah lies to me. "You stay quiet now.

You'll only go and get Poppa even more mad, and you know what he gets doin' when he's mad."

I bite down hard on my lip, tasting warm copper as Momma lifts herself into the back of the wagon. She waves at the two of us as the wagon pulls off, and we watch her sob and wave all the way down the road until she disappears.

"It's gonna be okay, Jesse," Jonah says. "We'll see Momma again someday. I promise. Until then, I'll look after—"

"You boys get inside. Now," Poppa says.

∽

JESSE OPENED HIS EYES. He tried to move and found himself unable. Every one of his limbs felt like lead, even his eyelids as he tried to blink. Soreness laid siege to his every sinew, and fatigue embraced him like none he'd ever felt. It brought a smile to his lips, even though that hurt like hell, too.

He was alive, damn it.

Jesse looked around and found he didn't recognize where he was. It looked like a doctor's quarters, but none he'd ever remembered setting foot in. But what did he remember? He could remember the dream, or was it a memory unlocked by the trauma he'd been through perhaps? He'd known who Lonnie Compton was after all: his mother's cousin. It made sense he would know where she was.

Across from him, a door opened, and in stepped somebody he did recognize: Dieter the doctor. The look of surprise on his face suggested he didn't expect to see Jesse awake.

"Mein Gott!" Dieter exclaimed. He rushed over to the bed and immediately brought a finger up to Jesse's face. Swinging it from side to side, Jesse's eyes followed it. "Jesse, can you hear me?"

"Of course, Doc," Jesse said. Well, he tried, but all that came out was a ragged whisper. The doctor left the cot briefly and then returned with a glass of water. Jesse took to it like a thirsty horse. "Ah! Sip. *Sip!*" Dieter said, before pulling the glass away. "Not too much in your frail state, mein freund. Alas, it is good to see you awake again. There will be a few here pleased to see you!"

"How... long?" Jesse eventually managed through what felt like a throat full of sawdust.

"You've been in a coma, Jesse. Nine days. Your friend has been by your side for all of them. He'll be kicking himself he's missed you wake up!" Dieter said with a laugh.

"F... friend?"

"Ya. Nodin. But anyway. Get some rest. I'll have some soup brought to you. You might not like the sound of this, but what you need right now, Jesse, is more sleep!"

The doctor was right. Jesse didn't like the sound of that. But his eyes were feeling heavy again. As he fought to keep them open, Jesse saw Jonah outside the window. His young older brother smiled, waved at him, and mouthed something; it looked like Jonah was saying 'goodbye Jess.' He fought off another blink and Jonah was gone.

Jesse soon found himself dreaming again.

～

Several days passed, with Jesse dipping in and out of consciousness. Sometimes for a minute or two, but as the days went on, he'd be awake for longer and longer. This morning, he was up, alert, and sitting upright on his cot. His body no longer felt made of lead, and he was grateful for the use of his arms again, which he used to hold the first cup of coffee he'd had in a fortnight. Sipping it, and feeling the burn as it ran down into his belly, he savored the bitter heat as if for the first time.

"A great cup of coffee, Greta. Thank you kindly," Jesse said, no longer having a mouth full of sawdust, too.

"Very welcome," Greta said sternly. It appeared even once you got to know her, she still spoke like she was irritated with the very sight of you. Dieter had told him it was a common thing among German women. She put a plate of fruit on a side table and left the doctor's office.

A moment later Nodin entered, carefully closing the door behind him. "I spoke to the butcher and his son."

"And?" Jesse asked.

"I explained why I loosed the arrows at his boy in the

forest. That it was the sight of the rifle that gave me cause, and I was never intending to hit. Only scare them off."

"And what did they say?"

"Nothing at first. The doctor was there too, which I was grateful for. Eventually, though, the butcher seemed… satisfied."

"See, I told you they'd come round. I reckon the whole camp is still a little shaken up by those mountain men."

"You would be correct."

Jesse scratched at the thickening beard on his chin, trying to quell an itch that was almost constant now. He couldn't wait to get a good shave. "There is something I keep meaning to ask you, Nodin. About what went down up at that shack."

"Then ask."

"When you tackled Otis. You saw that necklace around his neck. Why did it startle you the way it did?"

Nodin frowned. He dipped a hand in his pocket and produced the very necklace Jesse had mentioned. A thin leather strap, adorned with teeth; Jesse couldn't tell from what kind of animal. "My brother, not too much older than the doctor's boy, came out this way on a vision quest. A rite of passage for any man of the Crow Clan. When he did not return, I came out here to search for him… this…"

"Oh," Jesse said, regretting his asking. "I'm so sorry, Nodin."

"Do not be. It was not your fault. I thank you for killing the men responsible."

"Black Fang did most of the work on the older one," Jesse said.

"Somehow that does not surprise me. I believe you have Mother Nature's respect."

"I'll keep that in mind next time I plan a trip out in the wilds. I take it a party went out for Otis's body?"

Nodin nodded. "He was given a proper burial according to your God. I can not say that I agree with such respect shown to a man like that."

"I'd have left him for the wolves, too," Jesse said. He shuffled around on his bed and winced. "Goddamn, it still hurts to move. I'm gonna be here a while, aren't I?"

"The doctor seems to think so."

"Why?" A knock at the door answered Jesse. It opened and inside stepped the doctor. "Speak of the devil."

Dieter smiled sheepishly. "Apologies, gentlemen. I've been meaning to catch you, Jesse, about your recovery."

"I think Nodin may have beaten you to the bad news there, Doc," Jesse said. "I'm gonna be here a while."

"Yes, zat is true. But not just because of your recovery."

Jesse cocked his head and furrowed his brow. He didn't like the somber tone the Doc was taking; he liked even less the fact that he was now pulling up a chair to his cot. "What are you meaning here, Doc?"

"It is November. And while you need a few weeks

to recover, I'm afraid you won't be strong enough to travel soon enough. You see, up here in ze mountains, the winter is particularly tough as snow covers zis whole area, cutting Bleaker's Creek off from anybody else."

"That's fine. I'll borrow a horse and brave the cold."

"I cannot allow you to do zat, Jesse. Not even the horse would survive such harsh temperatures. I'm afraid you will be stuck here until spring."

Jesse frowned. "But... but I can't. I need to get to San Francisco. I got a girl waiting for me and I've already delayed too long and—"

"I'm sorry, Jesse. Truly I am."

"Oh, *hell*!" Jesse said. He bit down on his lip as he felt tears threaten at the corners of his eyes.

"Doctor, may I stay too?" Nodin asked.

"Why, of course, Nodin. But you'll have to get used to that bed of yours!" Dieter said, trying to lighten up the dour tone.

"Thank you," Nodin said. He then put a hand on Jesse's shoulder. "If you leave now, you will die. This time, I *will* stop you... friend."

Jesse looked up at Nodin and said, "Thank you."

"I will make my leave," Dieter said.

"Wait," Jesse said, clearing his throat. He took a deep breath and got a hold of himself. "I had a letter I was going to send to my girl, Winona."

"Yes, we found that on you. I'm afraid it was rather... soiled with blood."

"Never mind that," Jesse said. "Can I have some paper to write another? Is there time for that?"

"Of course. Dixie will be up in a few days for one last supply call. I'll have him take care of its posting for you in Missoula. I'll get you something to write with at once!"

"Thank you, Dieter."

"No problem, mein freund."

∽

Within days, the first of the snow began to fall.

Jesse had re-written his letter to Winona, detailing as much as he could about what had transpired since his last day with her. Twice now he had encountered obstacles in his path to her, and he imagined there would be more. The frontier, although much tamer than it was years ago, still had its dangers and its trepidations, and Jesse was not the kind of man to sit by and watch if he ever saw trouble. It was that very side of him that had thrust him into Winona's life in the first place. But it also meant he could not be sure exactly when he would see her; it might be months or even longer still.

He did make her a promise that he would get to her, though. No matter what, he would find a way. He still had his business with Lonnie Compton, but that would not delay him much, especially in comparison to the long stay he was forced to undertake at Bleaker's Creek. He only asked for her patience and wished her good health in the meantime.

Having finished the letter, he enclosed it in the envelope and handed it to Dieter. He then told the doctor that the writing had tired him and that he was going to try and sleep some more. The doctor bid Jesse goodbye and left him alone.

In truth, Jesse was not tired. While his hand did ache, and the thinking of what to write had started the drums pounding in his head again, he did not want to sleep. He merely wanted the solitude of the room, so that he could spare himself the embarrassment of witnesses to his tears.

INTERLUDE FOUR

When the snow fell in Bleaker's Creek, it fell heavily.

Nodin could not quite believe the sheer volume of the white that covered the camp; it was almost buried beneath it. Everybody in the Creek had relocated to the inn. Jesse had been carried over, despite his protests and adamant cries that he could have walked over himself. That was until he tired himself out from arguing so much.

In the days ahead, there was never much privacy. Nodin did not mind that, as it reminded him of the Crow: spending all their days together either in camp, or hunting and foraging. He often thought of his brother and dwelled on the sadness. It was a necessary part of grief. He spoke of him to Jesse and shared stories of what the two of them had done together. With each story told, the sadness dulled, and in its place, a sense of loving pride grew instead. Jesse often remarked on what a man his brother sounded like and regretted he had not had the chance to meet him. Nodin agreed. The two of them would have gotten along well, and Nodin told Jesse he would have made a great Crow, had he not been born white.

As the weeks passed, Jesse became more mobile, and even began to have the occasional drink. He claimed it was medicinal, to warm his bones and soothe his aching muscles. Nodin suspected otherwise, but the doctor did not protest.

One evening, the doctor's boy, Otto, sat with them. He did not say much, but Jesse's lips had been loosened by the whiskey. Eventually, Jesse got the boy talking about what he wanted to do with himself. Otto had said he wanted to be a doctor like his father and help people. But he was worried about the way he sounded and how people might treat him.

"You sound American to me, kid," Jesse had said. Nodin did not understand, as the boy's voice was very different. But Otto had smiled and, across from them at a table, so had his father.

∽

THEY PASSED their days with stories. Jesse would talk about his woman, Winona. She sounded to Nodin to be quite ferocious, who could, according to Jesse, "stand down the Devil himself when it came to winning an argument." A worthy partner for Jesse indeed.

Jesse had taught him a card game called 'poker.' Nodin had been slow to pick it up, not seeing the point of such arbitrary differences in cards and how a man could be so stupid as to lose his possessions over them. His opinion changed once he learned it was not the cards a man read, but the eyes of the man across from him. They played poker every day. Nodin enjoyed the game and its concept of bluffing, a foolish name for lying, but fun nonetheless. He had taught Jesse a few phrases of the Crow, but he was not so quick to pick up the language, and soon the pair of them found themselves indulging in more bluffing games of poker.

Christmas came around. The whites celebrated the birth of their God by giving each other gifts, another notion that struck Nodin as strange, especially as nobody had anything to give each other. Jesse had told him that the gift was what they had already been giving each other: time.

People sang songs, danced, and shared games with the children. Joan, the quiet woman they had saved from the mountain men, had stayed for the winter too. She had a most beautiful voice, singing wonderful songs that made no sense to him but were enjoyable in their melodies nonetheless.

More weeks passed. Jesse taught Nodin the ways of his

pistol, while Nodin showed Jesse the ways of the bow, a much more complex art than simply pointing a piece of steel and pulling a trigger. Jesse was slow to learn the patience, steadiness, and dexterity required for loosing an arrow (mostly because of his healing body), but they had time. And plenty of arrows.

"Where do you get your arrows?" Jesse had asked.

"Branches," Nodin had replied.

"Then how do you get them so straight?"

"You pick a straight branch."

Joan joined in too, and Jesse was grateful for the competition between them. Nodin had not laughed so much in years, watching Jesse's initial and embarrassing attempts.

Eventually, the temperatures rose and the snow began to thaw. Jesse was himself again, feeling rested, full of vigor, and mostly free of discomfort. Even the doctor was impressed at just how well he was. It was the night before they were due to leave Bleaker's Creak when Jesse turned to him. "Hey, Nodin," Jesse had asked. "Your name, what does it mean?"

"The wind," Nodin had said.

11

A LOT OF DAMNED NERVE

Jesse tightened the saddle on the horse and winced. He wasn't *quite* fully recovered yet.

"Are you sure you are okay to ride?" Nodin asked.

"Yes," Jesse said. "I've waited long enough." He looked up at the trees, their bare branches sprouting the beginnings of verdant leaves. "Now's as good a time as any to start moving again." Jesse turned to the waiting Dieter, Greta, and Otto.

The doctor reached out to shake Jesse's hand. "It has been a pleasure, Jesse."

"It's been all mine, Doc. I owe you my life."

"You owe it to your friend, too," Dieter said.

"Pretty sure me and he are even," Jesse said with a wink at Nodin. He huffed in response. In the distance, a stagecoach was departing. Joan called out goodbye from its window, and the group of them all waved back. "Will she be okay?" Jesse asked.

"I think so," Dieter said. "She's got a hard time of it, going home to break the news to her father-in-law. But she is committed to her return and continuation of her late husband's work."

"You'll keep an eye out for her when she's back here, right?"

"But of course!" Dieter said.

Red and Kip approached them. The pair of them made a beeline for Nodin, who stiffened as he turned to them. Red swallowed hard and nodded, before offering his hand to Nodin. He shook it, then did the same with the butcher's boy.

"Safe journey now, both o' you," Red said. He put an arm around his boy and the two of them left just as quickly as they came.

"Well, how about that?" Jesse said. "And on that note," he continued, tipping his ruined hat to everyone in turn while Nodin climbed onto the horse, "goodbye, everyone. And thank you all again. I'm most grateful."

"Goodbye, Jesse," Dieter said.

Jesse climbed up with Nodin's help, doing his best to hide the pain it caused him. The horse began its canter out of Bleaker's Creek and toward the home of Lonnie Compton.

Jesse took one last look back and waved.

～

It took about an hour to get to Lonnie's. Jesse could see the lodge, a big step up from the mountain men's shack. Thick logs secured its four walls under a thatched roof around a stone chimney spewing smoke. The thing was built to last, that was for sure. And somebody was most definitely home.

Nodin lowered Jesse off the horse.

"I got this, Nodin. You hang back, no need to spook him," Jesse said.

He walked up the path to the house, keeping an eye out for snares. Given his experience up in these mountains, he was not about to be complacent now. Jesse noted a small pen to the right of the house. A few goats ambled around inside the wooden fences. He saw a chicken coop, too. All the makings of a self-sufficient man.

"Take another step and you won't another," came a voice from the shadows in the doorway.

"Relax, I mean you no harm," Jesse said. He raised his hands above his head, as best as the niggling pain in his shoulders would allow him. "You Lonnie Compton?"

Jesse's answer came in the form of a double-barreled shotgun poking out of the shadows of the doorway. "Who the hell wants to know? And how the hell did you get my name?"

"A friend of mine gave it to me. My name... is Jesse Clayton."

The man stepped out of his doorway. Dressed in a soiled vest, he now sported a graying beard and a lot more wrinkles, but he was never growing back that missing half of his ear. It was Lonnie Compton all right. "You got a lot of damned nerve showing up here, Jesse."

"You know why I'm here, Lonnie. Give me what I need and I'll go on my way and leave you be. You can pretend like I was never even here, okay?"

"Where's your brother?"

"Dead."

Lonnie wheezed a laughed. "And good riddance, too."

"You ain't the first to be of that opinion."

Lonnie lowered the shotgun and started walking. "Come on now, let's get this done quick. I'll take you to her."

⁂

THERE SHE WAS, right in front of him. After all these years he'd waited to see her again and yet here he was, lost for words. The headstone stood in front of an oak tree, the kind Momma had always said had been her favorite on account of their lobed leaves. Jesse never really understood his mother's affection for a leaf, but he had always brought one home for her if he saw it. He also found it difficult to comprehend what he was seeing. Alberta Clayton, reduced to a name etched on a stone tablet stuck in the ground in Montana. So very far from where she had been his mother. And where they had both been home.

"You satisfied?" Lonnie asked. Jesse sensed an air of impatience. He was standing a few feet away, either out of respect or to keep some range on Jesse. Not that he cared.

What mattered to Jesse was that his mother was dead. He'd considered this possibility before and thought about the anger he would feel if he couldn't see her face again. It had been so long, he'd forgotten what she looked like. And now he'd never know, though he felt no swelling of fury within himself. Nor the compulsion for tears. Just a numbness in his fingers and a hollowness in his chest, as if there were now a hole in his heart.

"Let out with it, how did she die?" Jesse said softly.

"She was a lunger."

Jesse nodded. "How long ago?"

"Eleven years just this winter. It took hold of her quick, but long overstayed its welcome. She was lookin' to die a while."

Jesse's eyes daggered Lonnie. "And you let her suffer?" he said and absently put a hand to the Smith & Wesson.

"It was her choice to fight it," Lonnie said, already pointing the barrels at Jesse. "If you remember your momma putting up with yer daddy for as long as she did, you'll know it's just the kinda thing she'd do. I'm just glad she got to dyin' without seeing you two boys again, with what the two of you got up to."

"Things ain't always the way they're painted in the papers, Lonnie."

"Whatever you say. You might change your names, but them pictures don't lie."

"It was a long time ago."

"You're different now, is that it? Alberta'd be turnin' in her grave if she knew."

Jesse tipped his hat to the headstone. "Goodbye, Momma. Sorry I wasn't here. I love you." Jesse said quietly. He turned and started walking back toward Nodin and the horse. "Bye, Lonnie," Jesse called curtly.

Compton hawked and spat in Jesse's direction.

∼

Nodin pulled Jesse up onto the horse. He noted the somber look on Jesse's face. "Did it not go well?" he asked.

"We both lost somebody out here, Nodin. I think it's best we move on," Jesse said.

"I see," Nodin said. He tapped his heels into the horse's sides and off it began to trot.

They rode in silence for a few minutes and Jesse was grateful for the brief moment of quiet. Maybe he was in shock or perhaps somewhere deep down he had always known. Whatever the reason, Jesse Clayton knew that now was not the time to grieve his mother. He would, in time, he knew that. But for now, it was simply a fact that his mother was dead, nothing more. He had what he came here for. Now it was time to turn his attention back to Winona. And the rest of his life.

"You have made your visit to this Compton man, learned what you have. Where are we going now, then?" Nodin asked.

Jesse thought a moment. A question occurred to him. "*We*? Not to sound disrespectful, Nodin, but don't you have some place of your own to be?"

"I made a promise to the doctor: I would stay by your side until you were recovered and fully yourself again."

"I am myself again," Jesse protested.

"Says he who needs help to get on a horse. Once you can do that, maybe then I will leave."

"Well, okay then, Nodin," Jesse said. He couldn't help but grin.

"Where do we go now?"

"I'm thinking Missoula, but I guess wherever you take me, *Wind*."

EPILOGUE

"I thought you said there was poker in these places?" Nodin asked impatiently.

They were in the Silver Spur again on the west side of Missoula, not too far from the train station. They had another hour to kill before their train to Rathdrum was departing, so Jesse had opted that they spend their time with a drink or two to help speed up their waiting.

"Poker doesn't tend to happen until the evenings. Most folks are working right now. If you're that desperate, sure, we could find ourselves a gambling house. Gotta be one nearby. But tell me this: you got any money?"

Nodin shook his head. "I have not the need."

"Well, that makes two of us. I lost mine somewhere between the waterfall and the fightin' with those mountain men."

Nodin frowned. "But we did not play for money."

Jesse laughed. "Folks 'round here will. And they won't play for nothing else, especially with an Indian." As if to confirm Jesse's saying, two men entered the bar and immediately fixed their eyes on Nodin with a mix of distaste and unease. One of them put a hand to his knife. Jesse waved a hand and smiled at the two of them. The pair of them turned and left.

"You two gonna be here much longer? I'd prefer it if your dirt-eater wouldn't keep drivin' away my bid-ness," the barkeeper said. Judging by the size of his belly, Jesse supposed a slow hour on a Tuesday morning wouldn't hurt the man too much. He slapped a coin on the table and called for another round. The tender huffed and brought over the bottle, poured the drinks, and then snatched up the coin before scurrying away.

"Does it bother you, the looks you get?"

"Less so than when they try to kill me," Nodin said, sipping at his drink. Jesse went to take a sip of his when another man, this one with a large satchel, entered the bar.

"There a Jesse Clayton here?" he asked, wielding a letter. Jesse raised his hand and the man rushed over, delivering the letter. Jesse gave his thanks and the mailman moved on.

Jesse examined the letter, addressed to him at Dixie Rhode's place here in Missoula. Jesse flipped the envelope over to see the return address and the name of the sender:

Winona Squires

Jesse's heart quickened. It had been so long since those cold winter months when he had sent word to Winona that he had forgotten about it. The letter's origin puzzled him. According to the return address, Winona was not in San Francisco but was somewhere in Nevada. A little closer, but still, it was going to be a long ride once they got back into Idaho; there was no more money for train fares.

A problem for tomorrow, anyhow, Jesse thought.

He jabbed a finger into the corner of the envelope when once again the bar door swung open. In stepped a quartet of men, all dressed in matching attire. Black top hats and jackets, and pinstripe trousers tucked into muddied black riding boots. Jesse lowered his hand under the table, resting it on the Smith & Wesson. Jesse knew that uniform.

Behind them, another man, clad in a grey duster, stepped into the bar. The uniformed men stepped aside to allow this man to pass. His strides were long and determined. He paused to look around the bar through hawk-like eyes. He looked to be on the good side of forty, with his cropped black hair graying around the ears. The man settled his attention on Jesse, smiled in a way that gave Jesse pause, then looked to the men with him and gave directions.

Two of the men held shotguns across their waists. They were posted on either side of the entrance. Another was sent around the perimeter of the bar. Jesse watched him as he finally settled himself by the rear entrance. The fourth, the oldest and least threatening-looking of the group, approached Jesse and Nodin's table. He stopped a few feet away from Nodin, who was readying his blade. Jesse shook his head. If there was a fight to be had, bullets would already be flying. This was a show of force, nothing but spectacle bravado.

The man in the duster approached, walking right up to the table and addressing Jesse directly. "Jesse Clayton?" he asked.

"That's me."

"You are a difficult man to find."

"Maybe you and your friends there just weren't lookin' hard enough," Jesse said.

"Indeed. In any case, I'll get right to it in the interest of haste. My name is Patrick Flynn." Up close, Jesse could see the man was handsome for his age. Cleanly shaven, with angular looks starting to lose themselves in loosening skin. Flynn had a firm quality to his voice and was very careful to enunciate each word perfectly. "I work for Ellis Osborne."

"Ellis Osborne? Now, why does that name ring a bell?" Jesse said, knowing full well who Osborne was.

"That business on the train a few months back? It was the robbery of his money which you attempted to foil. I'm sure you remember," Patrick said. Jesse detected an undercurrent in the man's voice. Was it impatience or irritation?

"Ah, yes," Jesse said. "If he's looking for recompense for not saving his money, tell him I'm sorry but I just spent my last dollar."

"Mr. Osborne does not seek money, Mr. Clayton. He seeks your help."

"Really?" Jesse said, leaning back in his chair. "With what exactly?"

"The safe retrieval of a great interest to him."

Jesse nodded slowly. "Can't trust your Pinkerton friends here with something like that?" Jesse looked around at the armed men surrounding them. "One thing that strikes me as a mite odd, though. You boys seem a little too well-armed for me to think he's *just* asking. It leads me to think: what are your instructions should I refuse?"

Flynn leaned forward and clasped his hands together on the table. Jesse noticed the fine white-leather gloves he wore. "We are permitted to use... more *persuasive* means," Flynn said.

"That doesn't sound legal," Jesse said. Slowly, he pointed his gun toward Flynn under the table.

Flynn smiled unpleasantly. "Mr. Osborne understands the law is open to interpretation out here."

Maybe there was more to this than a show of force. This Patrick Flynn was both impatient and irritated. The man felt like his time here was a wasted effort, that much Jesse could tell. He wanted out of here as soon as he could, with or without Jesse. Jesse was of a mind that Patrick Flynn may prefer to leave empty-handed. "Just what is this *great interest*, then?" Jesse asked.

"I am not permitted to say at this juncture, Mr. Clayton," Flynn said.

"Why not?" Jesse asked.

"My orders are to ensure you embark upon Mr. Osborne's locomotive," Flynn stated, almost as if he were reciting the words.

"You can just say if you don't know, Patrick. I can call you Patrick, right?"

"You can call me *Mr. Flynn*. Now, will you come willingly?" Flynn said. The firmness in his voice took on a more sour tone.

Good, Jesse thought. "Apologies, Mr. Flynn," he said, exchanging a glance with Nodin. The two had bonded in those winter months, and Clayton knew that look in his eyes. He was ready to follow Jesse's lead, whatever happened.

The problem was that there was a lot of distance between them and the three at the door. If Jesse took out Flynn, they'd need to find cover. There was no way he was taking down three gunfighters at this range before one of them plugged him and Nodin. Not only that, but in the winter months of teaching Nodin to shoot, Jesse had noticed his aim was severely off. It had improved, but the stiffness in his shoulder still gave Jesse pause on his ability in a gunfight.

Jesse kept his cool. "You know, I'm a little tired of trains. How about my partner and I think on it a little first?"

Flynn sighed. "I don't have time for this," he said as he raised a hand and closed it into a fist.

Jesse looked again to Nodin, just as the agent behind him produced a blackjack. The agent swung the weapon, clattering the leather club into the back of Nodin's head. His eyes rolled back as he slumped forward. His whiskey glass jumped as Nodin crashed onto the table.

Jesse went to draw his weapon, but Flynn had already drawn his, a long-barreled Colt which was now pointed right at Jesse's head.

"Take Clayton. We don't need the other one," Flynn said to the agent who had felled Nodin. He now pulled Jesse unceremoniously from his chair.

"If you hurt him, I'll—"

"Do what, exactly?" Flynn said, articulating every bit of glee he felt in this turn of events. Flynn nodded to the agent next to Jesse. "I don't want to hear him again."

Jesse turned just as the blackjack came down on him.

Printed in Great Britain
by Amazon